When the Bough Breaks

ALSO BY ANNA MYERS

Red-Dirt Jessie

Rosie's Tiger

Graveyard Girl

Fire in the Hills

Spotting the Leopard

The Keeping Room

Ethan Between Us

When the Bough Breaks

Anna Myers

Walker & Company
New York

First published in the United States of America in 2000
by Walker Publishing Company, Inc.

Published simultaneously in Canada by Fitzhenry and
Whiteside, Markham, Ontario L3R 4T8

Library of Congress Cataloging-in-Publication Data
available upon request.

ISBN: 0-8027-8725-8

Book design by Jennifer Ann Daddio

Printed in the United States of America

2 4 6 8 10 9 7 5 3 1

This book is dedicated to the people who helped through the illness and death of Paul Myers, who was my husband for thirty years.

First, to my brothers and sisters, both those who are related by blood and those who were, in the beginning, in-laws. I cannot imagine what I would do without you.

Thank you to my nieces and nephews. I am lucky to have such loving, thoughtful young people in my life. Becky, thank you for staying beside us every step of the journey.

Thank you to Rose and Wendell Myers, who were Paul's parents and who are now mine. You worried about me when your own hearts were breaking.

Thank you to the administrators, faculty, and staff of Chandler Public Schools. You went far beyond the duty of colleagues. You showed me love and support in so many ways. I love you all and treasure the memories of working with you.

Thank you to Paul's coworkers at the Oklahoma Employment Service. You did so much to make Paul's last days easier, and you did so much to make his work days happy.

Thank you to the employees of Oklahoma City Veterans' Hospital and to the people in Paul's classes there. He loved working with you, and I believe he knows about the garden you planted and the book sales in his memory.

Thank you to Murl Smith and Don Broyles for taking care of so many details. We counted on you.

Thank you to Jim Ross for being his friend and for knowing you still are.

Thank you to Marilyn Hoover, Sylvia Janes, and Jayne Mays. You stood beside me in the halls and in my life. Thank you for being with us that last day.

Thank you to my lifelong friend, Darlene Crofford, for holding my hand and giving me your house key.

Thank you to Beverly and Bob McBride for coming so far when we needed you and coming again to carry him.

Thank you to Linda and Lowell Jansen. Linda, your faith was a light. Lowell, I'll always be glad your hand was on his head, and I'll always be grateful for the eulogy, your last gift to your buddy.

Thank you to David and Martha Evans. You postponed your lives to sit with us day after day at the hospital through the long summer. You were never far away during the heartbreak of fall and winter or during my lonely spring.

I wish I could list all of you who prayed for us, sent flowers or donations in Paul's name, brought food, called with kind words, or just squeezed my hand in the grocery store. So many, many people let us know you cared. I hope I won't leave anyone out, but I want to say thank you to the following people who found special ways to help: Pastor Rick Blackwell and his congregation at Chandler's First Baptist Church, youth of Chandler's First Christian Church, Jan Branson, my cousins Edmond and Clara Eaton, Molly Griffis, Kate Gulley, Judy Hill, Julie Hovis, teachers at Broken Arrow's Leisure Park Elementary, Brad Milburn, Bill and Nelda Matthews, Glen and Aurilla Reeder, Charlene and Ben Sasser, Nathan Sain, Pat Wade, members of Tulsa Night Writers, Doris Wheelus.

Most of all, thank you to my children, Ginny Myers, Anna-Maria Myers, and Ben and Mandy Matthews. No man was ever more proud of his kids than your father was. He lives in you, and I couldn't live without you.

When the Bough Breaks

1.

There was forever the water. "If you drink from the Ridge Fork, you will always return," the old people liked to say, and it was the water that held Portia McKay. At first she splashed at the shallow edge with her sister Carolina, two little girls, laughing. Later, on that terrible night, the water called to her, roaring over the rock and swelling over the banks. And as an old, old woman she sat by the water's edge, sat on the great rock and remembered.

The water pulled the new girl, Ophelia, along the mountain road that was little more than a trail. When finally the house came into view, she stopped beside the big pine tree to look at it. "It's been there always," Mrs. Reynolds, her new foster mother, had told her, "and old Miss McKay right there in it. Never slept a night in any other place, they say. Didn't even want a phone when they finally got the lines in up here. Peculiar old thing, she is, but she won't hurt you none. And the pay's good."

Mrs. Reynolds had looked at Ophelia as she spoke. The muscles around the woman's mouth twitched, and Ophelia saw what she thought might be a smirk about to form. She turned her back. She had to live in this foster home. The caseworker had said they would not move her again. If she had to live here, it would be better not to imagine that her foster mother smiled about how old Miss McKay could not be more peculiar than Ophelia herself.

Now, standing beside the pine, Ophelia took a deep breath. It was not fear that made her stop. What could there be about an old house or an old lady to scare her? Ophelia did not fear much, not anymore. She paused only to rest, her breaths coming in short gulps. She had moved too quickly along the hillside trail.

Mrs. Reynolds had not mentioned the reading job until Ophelia had cleared the table after supper. "You want to be heading over to Miss McKay's?" she had asked. "She's the spinster woman lives just up the hill a piece. She's paid my foster girls in the past to read out loud to her." Mrs. Reynolds had cocked her head to study Ophelia. "You can read good, can't you? They never said you had any troubles with your books and such."

"I can read," Ophelia said. She did not tell Mrs. Reynolds that she had taught herself to read before she went to school, that she had taken books from her older brother's bag, that at five she could read as well as Roy could at ten. Mrs. Reynolds had gone on talking about old Miss McKay and her house. Ophelia kept thinking about Roy, but she said nothing. She would never tell Mrs. Reynolds anything about Roy, not anything at all.

Portia McKay paused by the front window. "The girl's come to read." She spoke aloud to herself. There had been no one else to talk to for years, not even while her father lived. She did not actually see Ophelia, who was still among the thick trees, but Portia knew when a human came on her place. Deer, raccoons, even bobcats visited unnoticed because Portia had long since given up keeping dogs, resenting how they died of old age and left her. But people did not often come, and Portia McKay sensed when someone was near.

She opened the screen door, and as the girl moved into her view, Portia sucked in her breath. The girl was blond, the shiny hair blowing against the white skin and rosy cheeks. "A golden girl," Portia whispered to herself, and the familiar pain shot through her. It was the pain she always felt when she saw a beautiful blond girl.

For a moment she considered sending the girl away, calling out to her that she had changed her mind, that she no longer desired to be read to. Instead she held the door open. There had been no reader for five months while the Reynoldses had a foster boy in their care. Portia would not have a boy in her house.

Ophelia watched as the front door opened. In the dim late-day light, she saw a figure come out to stand on the screened porch. The woman was tall and very straight. Ophelia had expected a bent, little old lady. "She's old as Methuselah," Mrs. Reynolds had said. Ophelia had wondered who Methuselah was, but she had not asked. Ophelia never asked questions and never volunteered information.

"Come in, child," the woman called. "What's your name?"

"Ophelia," the girl said when she stood inside. "My name is Ophelia." She never volunteered a last name unless asked directly.

"Well!" Portia closed the door and studied the girl closely. "We have something in common, both with names from Shakespeare. My given name is Portia. Of course, you'll call me Miss McKay. Ophelia's not a common name. How did you come to have it?"

Ophelia hated questions. She looked down. "My mother gave it to me. She loved Shakespeare."

Your mother's dead, then, Portia thought, noting the past tense. She noticed, too, the way the girl said the word "mother." "You loved your mother very much, didn't you?" She surprised herself with the question. Portia, like her visitor, did not often invite personal discussion.

"Yes." She might not mind talking to this old woman, she thought. "Did your mother name you?"

"No," said Portia. "My father chose the name." She said no more, but still, the memory, that first memory, could not be stopped. Why, she wondered, had she been cursed with such a mind, one that even after more than eight decades could still see the little girls, her sister and herself.

Portia was dark and smaller than her blond sister. Lina held Portia's hand and watched her little sister's eyes. She squeezed Portia's hand if the lids dropped over the brown eyes.

The girls sat on a wooden bench. Their feet did not touch the floor, but their backs were straight. Papa did not allow slouching during the recitation. "This is Shakespeare," he said that night, the night of Portia's earliest memory. "You, Portia, were named for the character who made this speech."

Portia had sat up straight, but she did not look at her father. Instead she studied the shiny black shoes that covered her dangling feet.

"The quality of mercy is not strained," Father had said. Father talked a lot about mercy, quoting the words Shakespeare had given the character Portia. As a little girl, she did not understand her papa's words, but she remembered them always against the sound of wind in the mountain pines and the cry of a lone bobcat.

Portia shook her head. There was no time to go over memories now. The girl waited. "Well," she said, "come on in and let's get started."

Ophelia followed her into the living room of the big house. The walls were lined with filled bookshelves, more books than the girl had ever seen except in a library.

Above the fireplace was a portrait of a man in an old-fashioned suit. He had gray hair and a stern, unsmiling face.

"That," said Miss McKay, nodding toward the picture, "is Seth McKay, my father. He built this house and bought these books. But he won't be telling us what to read." She walked to stand before the books and was surprised to hear herself go on. "I have no likeness of my mother to show you. I wish I did." She turned back to study Ophelia. "I am told she had fair hair and skin like yours. My sister favored my mother, but I resemble my father."

Ophelia glanced again at the portrait. Yes, the eyes were the same, cold and hard. Miss McKay's hair was gray, but her dark skin indicated that the hair, too, had probably once been dark. Ophelia hoped the daughter had not inherited her father's personality. One look at the man's picture told Ophelia that she would have been afraid of Seth McKay.

"Here," said Portia McKay. "I haven't heard any Shakespeare for a long time. The last two girls were not good enough readers, but I have a feeling you are."

The book the old woman held was *Hamlet,* an orange book exactly like the one Ophelia had taken from a library years before. She fought down the memory. She needed to concentrate if she was to read Shakespeare aloud.

"You sit there near the lamp," Portia handed Ophelia the book, then pointed toward a small couch. "I'll sit in the rocking chair." She moved toward a large antique chair with worn arms and a brocade seat. "This was my father's chair. He allowed no one else to sit in it, ever." She turned her head to look up at the portrait above the fireplace. "But, as I said, he's dead now." She smiled and lowered herself onto the cushion.

Ophelia's hand shook as she opened the book. It had been five years since she read *Hamlet* on the floor of her first foster home, but she still remembered where the part about Ophelia's drowning was, near the end. She turned to the last page and began to flip pages backward.

"What are you doing?" Portia McKay leaned forward, her dark eyes boring into the girl.

Ophelia looked down at the book. How many hours of reading aloud would it take to find the part? She couldn't wait that long.

"I was just looking for the part about how Ophelia died. You know, the character I'm named for." The girl looked closely at the wrinkled, no-nonsense face and the dark eyes that did not look away. They were not cruel eyes. "I've always wanted to ask someone. Do you think Ophelia killed herself? I mean, did she go up in that tree and fall out on purpose?"

"I haven't read *Hamlet* in at least fifteen years, maybe longer." Portia leaned back in the chair. "When did you last read the play?"

Ophelia did not usually like to give information about herself, but there was something about this woman, something that would not let her lie or avoid, something that almost made her want to talk. "I read it when I was ten—five years ago."

"Ten? My goodness, did your mother read it with you?"

"My mother is dead. She died five years ago." Ophelia looked down. "She died before I read *Hamlet*."

"I see. So you read it all alone?" There was no sympathy in her words.

Ophelia liked the fact that Portia McKay did not sound sorry for her. Ophelia did not trust people who pretended to be sorry for her.

"I do everything alone."

"But you asked me a question. Asking questions is not a solitary activity."

"I want to know. I've wanted to know for a long time." She shrugged her shoulders. "No one else ever talked to me about *Hamlet*."

"Well, then find the page." She waved her hand in Ophelia's direction. "Go ahead, find it and read it to me." Portia McKay sat patiently while Ophelia scanned the pages.

"Here it is, on page two thirty-five."

There on the pendant boughs her coronet weeds
Clamb'ring to hang, an envious sliver broke.
When down her weedy trophies and herself
Fell in the weeping brook. . . .

"Well," said Portia, "Shakespeare certainly doesn't say it was on purpose. Ophelia was, of course, out of her mind." She closed her eyes and breathed out deeply. "People do strange things when they are out of their mind with fear."

"Fear? What was Ophelia afraid of?"

"Oh, I didn't mean to say fear. I suppose with Ophelia it was grief. Grief can do terrible things to a person's mind, too."

Ophelia closed the book. "Thank you," she said. "I'm really glad she didn't want to kill herself."

"You poor child. It has bothered you, hasn't it, thinking the character you're named for killed herself?"

This time Ophelia did not answer. She had already opened up too much to this woman.

Portia McKay did not need an answer. "I don't think Ophelia committed suicide." The old woman leaned close toward the girl again. "But you hear me, child. Stay away from that river you pass on the way here. We've had lots of rain in these parts lately. That river's full now, and its waters can be mean, even evil—mighty, mighty evil!"

Ophelia looked at the woman. Why should she be afraid of the water? Why should the woman care about her? She turned the book's pages back to the front. "Should I start to read now?" she asked.

Portia nodded, and Ophelia began: " 'Bernardo: Who's there? Francisco: Nay, answer me: Stand, and unfold yourself.' " She settled back in the couch and lost herself in the words.

"Enough," Portia said after almost an hour. "You will do nicely, quite nicely." She stood and led the way to the door. "Good-bye," she said crisply, and she held the door.

On the front step, Ophelia let her breath go out in a deep sigh. She could think about *Hamlet* now, think about her name. She crossed the bare brown earth of the yard, too shaded to have grass. With each step, memories came flooding back.

Ophelia could not remember when she had been told that she was named for a character from Shakespeare. She did remember the exact day when she asked her mother to tell her about the character for whom she was named.

M ama stood in front of her easel, but she held no paintbrush. She only looked at yesterday's work, not that Mama would have minded being interrupted by Ophelia. Mama was like that, gentle eyes smiling even after the sadness in them couldn't be hidden.

"Tell me about her, Mama, tell me about the Ophelia you named me for." Ophelia settled in the rocking chair, ready for her mother to talk.

"She was lovely, like you." Mama straightened the tubes of paint on the table beside her easel. "There was a boy named Hamlet, a fine boy who loved his parents very much, and he loved Ophelia." Mama turned away from the paints and looked at her daughter, who could remember well the sadness in those blue eyes.

"Maybe I shouldn't have chosen the name for you, but I thought it was so beautiful. Besides, in those days, when Roy was just little and we were considering names for our new baby, life was so good. I never worried about bad things."

Ophelia stood up and inched away from the chair back toward the door. "What do you mean, Mama? Why do you think maybe you shouldn't have named me Ophelia?"

Mama shook her head and made her voice light. "Oh, it's just silly. I'm glad I named you Ophelia. What happened to Shakespeare's character doesn't have anything to do with you." Mama held out her arm to put around Ophelia's shoulder. "Come on, we'll go sit by the fireplace, and I'll tell you all about Ophelia and Hamlet."

Ophelia did not move to her mother. She stepped back again. She did not want to hear something sad about the girl who had her name. "It's okay," she said. "You go ahead and paint. I've got homework. Maybe you should tell me later."

But later had never come. That Sunday evening when Ophelia had been ten was their last evening together. Ophelia and her mother had never again sat by the fire on a winter evening or on the porch on a summer afternoon to watch children play or the occasional car move down the quiet street of their little town.

When it was all over and she was settled in that first horrible foster home, Ophelia asked permission to walk the three blocks to the public library. It was still winter, and while she walked snow began to fall on her nose.

"Where are the Shakespeare books?" she asked the lady behind the big counter.

The woman gave her a questioning look. "Are you looking for one of the rewritten versions? We have a few of those. They're easier to read, you know."

Ophelia shook her head. "I want the real one, please," but after she had followed the librarian's directions to the shelf, she hesitated before reaching for *Hamlet*. Maybe she should let it go. What difference did it make now what happened to that other Ophelia? What difference did anything make with Mama gone? Ophelia almost turned away, but then she put out her hand for the orange book.

That night she lay still in the bed she shared with another foster girl, and she waited. The girl beside her slept, breathing evenly, but across the room in the single bed another girl rolled about.

When finally the room was quiet, Ophelia slipped

from her bed, took one of the quilts that had covered her, found her book, and crept to the bedroom door. "I'll leave the hall light on," the foster mother had told her, "in case you need to find the bathroom."

Ophelia settled beside the door and leaned against the wall. A thin ray of light came through the slightly open door, and she held her book so that the lines were illuminated a few at a time.

The words were hard to understand, and Ophelia wondered if she should have taken the librarian's easier version. She whispered the words aloud to herself, because hearing them seemed to help her understand. Hamlet, she discovered, was a prince whose father had been murdered, but it was only the unhappy Ophelia who mattered.

By reading and rereading, Ophelia made out the story. Hamlet had been in love with Ophelia, but after the trouble with his father, he lost interest. Then Ophelia's father got killed, and Ophelia lost her mind.

Ophelia put her book down and drew the quilt closer around herself. She knew how the girl felt about her father's death. Maybe, she thought, it would have been nice to lose her mind as Shakespeare's character had.

That other Ophelia had made a ring of flowers to put on her head and climbed up into a tree above water, and the branch she stepped on broke. Had Ophelia killed herself? Did she step on the branch on purpose? No, that didn't make sense. If she had wanted to drown herself, wouldn't she just have jumped into the water?

Ophelia put the book down and closed her eyes. So that was it. Mama hadn't wanted to tell her that Ophelia fell into a brook. Drowning wasn't so bad. It was certainly better than being torn up by a rifle, wasn't it? Ophelia had determined to watch for creeks or rivers in the town where she first became a foster child.

2.

Leaving the big house, Ophelia let her breath go out in a deep sigh. She had actually enjoyed reading Shakespeare's words aloud. She was so much better at it now than she had been at ten. Ophelia loved reading, loved words, but the old woman made her uncomfortable. Not at first, but when they had talked about whether or not Shakespeare's character had killed herself.

Why did she feel so drawn to this old woman? Ophelia did not want to open up to anyone. She did not want to care about anyone, not ever again.

Ophelia paused under the big pine at the edge of the yard where she had stood before going into the house, and she turned back to look.

There in the window was old Miss McKay, straight

and tall. Just exactly how old was the woman, anyway? Ophelia wondered. Why did her figure there in the window seem so strong? Why did she feel that the woman already had some sort of hold on her?

Ophelia swung quickly back. She did not want to look at Portia McKay. Even more, she did not want Portia McKay to look at her. The woman could see inside her. Ophelia hadn't let anyone get that close in a long time, not since she had lost Mama and Daddy and Roy.

She did not hurry down the path. She had always hurried home to Mama, but there was no rush to get to a foster home. After a few feet, she paused again. She could not see the river through the trees, but its rush filled her ears and seemed to pull her in that direction.

"Stay away from that river," Portia McKay had said, and her words had been powerful. If the old woman had stood beside her, Ophelia would never have left the path, but the water called to her as she pushed her way between the trees and through the tall, dead grass and blackberry vines.

Then just to her left she saw a path narrowly winding up to the road. Someone made trips to the river from the road, made them often enough to wear the grass away from the brown soil. "Oh," Ophelia said, sucking in her breath with surprise. Before her the Ridge Fork

River roared over the rocks at its bottom. "Evil" was how Miss McKay had described the water, but the river Ophelia saw was beautiful.

In the western part of the state where she had lived with her family she had not known a river, but in foster homes in the central part of Oklahoma she had ridden across rivers in cars. Those rivers were red colored and not at all appealing, but this river sparkled even in the shadows of late evening.

On the bank, just to her left, was a big rock. At its base was a flat rock about two feet long. The big rock might be a perfect spot to sit. Maybe she would even be able to reach the water with her feet. Inside her shoes her toes began to feel dry and hot. Wouldn't it be nice to dangle her feet in the water for a little while?

The path made reaching the rock easy, and in just a few minutes Ophelia's socks and shoes were off. Her legs were just long enough to comfortably reach the water.

The September sun had already set, and the rushing river seemed cold to her hot feet. Still, she plunged them in, drawing her body tight against the first biting shock.

After the original jolt, her feet felt good, and she settled into the slight indentation of the rock. It felt comfortable, like a well-worn chair. How deep was the water? she wondered. Probably fairly deep now, from what Miss McKay had said. Ophelia glanced down at the rock upon which she sat. Maybe during drier days this rock was not at the exact edge of the water.

She loved the sound of the water over the rocks, loved the wet smell that surrounded her. Someone else must love this water too. Someone else came often down that path to sit on this rock.

Ophelia looked back over her shoulder. What if that person came now? What if he or she came quietly down the path and Ophelia did not know until a hand reached out to touch her? She shuddered. Ophelia did not trust people, and she certainly did not want anyone sneaking up behind her. She pulled her feet out, shaking water off them as she reached for her socks.

She was about to slide off the rock when her fingers felt the line chiseled into the stone. Even before she looked, her fingers had found other marks—numbers or letters.

The late-evening light was not good there among the trees. For a moment she could not make out the numbers carved deeply into the dark stone, but then she was certain. *1921*, it said, and above the numbers there was more. *July 19, 1921.* Someone had etched a date into the rock. Had the rock been marked on that date almost eighty years earlier? Had someone sat long ago where she sat now and written that date?

Ophelia pulled her mind away from the date and slid off the rock. It was not her practice to go wondering about other people's lives. "Leave them alone and hope they leave you alone." She repeated the familiar words aloud to herself and started up the path away from the river.

By the time she reached her foster home, dark had come to the hillside, but a full, orange moon lit her way. Ophelia did not fear the night. For five years now night had been her favorite time. At night she was allowed to go to bed early. Sometimes her dreams were bad, but sometimes she dreamed of the early days when most of life had been easy and she had been loved. During the day there were no good times, and she had to put up with people, kids at school who stared at her rudely and sometimes did much worse.

She disliked the teachers, too, even the kind ones who smiled at her and tried to draw her out with writing assignments with sentences like "Sometimes I feel . . ." that she was supposed to finish. She did not do the assignments, and she did not smile back at the teachers.

At the door, she paused. She always found it hard to

walk into a foster home without knocking, but usually if she did knock, the foster parents would fuss and say, "This is your home now." She hated hearing that lie worse than she disliked walking in. She pulled at the storm door, but it was locked.

"Good," she said to herself, and she knocked hard on the door's metal frame.

"I'm coming," called Mrs. Reynolds, her heavy feet making thuds on the floor. "Lands," she said when she opened the door. "I completely forgot about you being out when I latched this. I'm sorry."

"It doesn't matter," said Ophelia. She stepped past Mrs. Reynolds into the living room.

The woman stayed at the door, looking out into the night. "Don't know why I always start to feel uneasy when it starts to get dark. Like my mother always said, 'There ain't nothing out there after dark except what was there in the light.' " She closed the door behind Ophelia and locked it. "Still, I don't feel easy inside after night comes to these hills. Maybe it's the sounds." She pushed back the curtain on the window near the door. "I think that's it. Sounds at night, they just give me the shivers."

"I don't want to go back to read to that woman." Ophelia moved on into the living room without looking back at her foster mother. "Do I have to? Are you going to make me go back there?" She whirled now to face the woman.

"Gracious." Mrs. Reynolds lifted her apron to wipe at her round face. "I don't know as I'd know how to make you do much of anything. I am, naturally, hoping you'll just sort of want to go to school, help out a little here, and generally behave yourself. But, no, I don't expect to do no fussing if you don't want to pick up pocket money by reading."

Ophelia bit at her lip. She had forgotten about the money. She wanted the money, wanted to add it to the little she had managed to save in the past. Then maybe someday she would have enough for a bus ticket home.

3.

〜

Portia McKay fried potatoes for her supper. It was a
rare day when she did not eat something fried. Her
father, too, had eaten that way and had died eleven
years earlier at the age of 105. Portia smiled as she
stirred the potatoes. If fried foods were the secret to
her father's long life, maybe she should give them up.
At ninety-two she was still strong and firm, but by one
hundred even her father had grown infirm. There would
be no one to take care of her as she had cared for her
father.

She ate the potatoes with the last green pepper from
her garden. Portia never used the dining room, with its
heavy formal furniture, now that her father was gone.
Instead she ate her meals at the small kitchen table that
gave her a view of the yard. Looking out was important

to Portia, who felt grateful that old age had only taken away the ability to see, even with glasses, the small up-close words of books.

Summer's grip on the mountainside was loosening. She studied the post oak tree near the window. In a couple of weeks October would arrive and bring its yellow paint to the tree. Her eyes moved to the tall pine farther away from the house. She studied the way the tree leaned with the wind, growing in the direction of the gust. "You're smart, tree," she murmured. If only her father had known how to bend with the wind. "Well," she added aloud, "you didn't bend so dadgum well yourself."

Next she noticed the cluster of goldenrod that grew close to the front doorstep, golden like the girl Ophelia. What was the child's last name? Portia wrinkled her forehead, trying to remember. *She didn't say, did she?* No, Portia was certain there had been no mention of a last name.

She ate the last bite of potato and moved with her plate and fork to the sink. Using hot water and soap to wash one plate, a fork, and a skillet seemed wasteful. Portia had been trained never to be wasteful, but she had also been trained never to leave dirty dishes. She had found delight in breaking some of her father's rules.

Others were too deeply ingrained to be buried with the old man's body.

Dishes and habits could fill her thoughts only briefly. The girl kept creeping back into her mind. How old was the girl? Portia wondered. She hadn't asked Bernice Reynolds when the woman brought word that a new foster girl had arrived.

Portia rarely made any inquiries of Bernice, who was the older woman's only real contact with the outside world. Five years before, when her last car had worn out, Portia had decided not to buy another one. She was getting too old to react quickly behind the wheel, and so she could no longer drive to town, six miles down the mountain.

Instead she paid her neighbor Bernice Reynolds to pick up supplies for her. Bernice, by nature a talkative woman, would have been glad to bring news with the bags of groceries, sharing whose house had burned, what banker had divorced his wife, who had won the race for mayor.

Portia McKay had squelched Bernice on the first deliver. "Never have been much for chitchat," the older woman said, and she turned her back on Mrs. Reynolds. Occasionally through the years Portia had been forced to remind her neighbor, always using the same words.

Portia reached for the dish towel hanging above her sink. Probably Bernice would think it was strange if now, after years of silence, she would suddenly start inquiring about the foster girl. The Reynoldses had lived down the hill from her for twelve years, and for ten years off and on Bernice had sent foster girls up the hill to read aloud. She would certainly wonder if Portia began asking questions about Ophelia.

Still, Portia really wanted to know about the girl whose face stirred memories for the woman. If she did not get information from Bernice Reynolds, there would, in all likelihood, be no information. In Ophelia, Portia knew, she had met a person as private, as unwilling to take part in chitchat, as Portia herself.

Portia moved again to the window. It was growing dark now. Yet she moved toward the door. The water called to her. She would go to sit on the rock. Night would be in full force before she reached the river. From the stand beside the door, Portia took a walking stick. She needed no help in the daytime, but at night she might step into a hole or stumble on a rock.

Falling was the only fear the night brought to Portia.

Darkness was her friend. It had been dark on July 19, 1921, when she had carved the date into the rock.

Ophelia decided not to think about Portia McKay. She would read to the old woman, at least until her wages could buy a bus ticket. Ophelia looked around her tiny room. The size did not trouble her. In fact, it was the best one she had ever had in a foster home. There was space only for a twin bed and one small chest. There would be no roommate. Another girl might come to take the equally small adjacent room recently vacated by a boy who was returned to his parents, but she would not get into Ophelia's life. Ophelia knew how to close doors.

"You can do your homework at the kitchen table," Mrs. Reynolds had told the girl when showing her the room. "There just ain't no space for a desk in here."

Ophelia chose instead to sit cross-legged on the bed, her paper for written work balanced on a book. Earlier she had tossed her books on the bed, but homework would have to wait. First she went to the chest, opened the top drawer, and took out a small, paperback atlas. She had sneaked it out of the library from a school she had attended last year when her plan to go home had first started to form.

She pushed aside her books and settled on the bed. Opening the atlas, she reached for a pencil and chewed on it while studying the map. A red dot marked home, Deer Run, a small town way out in western Oklahoma, almost to Texas.

From there they had taken her first to Arnett, the county seat. She had ridden in a sheriff's car, huddled near the door, her hand over her mouth to hold back the vomit that threatened to rise from her churning stomach.

If she closed her eyes, Ophelia could see herself in that car, could feel herself in that car, ten years old and terror stricken. If she let the picture stay in her mind, the vomit would start to rise again. For five years, Ophelia had been always close to vomiting.

In Arnett she had met Brenda Phillips, the case-worker, who hugged her. The sickness still threatened to come, but Brenda held her until Ophelia's body at last stopped the convulsive shaking. "We'll take you back to Deer Run to your grandmother's," Brenda had said.

But Grandma didn't want to keep Ophelia. "I'm too old," she said. "Besides, she would be better off somewhere away from Deer Run, someplace where people don't know the terrible story."

Ophelia hated to leave Grandma, but she did not cry when Brenda Phillips drove her away. She did not even look back at Grandma's house from the car window. Ophelia had decided not to cry anymore. Besides, maybe it really would be best to be in a strange town, where no one knew.

"We've found a home for you up in Harper County," Brenda told her. They had stopped at a drive-in restaurant, and Ophelia kept pulling on the straw of her root beer. "I don't usually have kids out of this county." Brenda paused to take a sip from her paper cup.

Ophelia said nothing, but she held her breath. She liked Brenda Phillips, liked the hugs even though she never hugged back, liked Brenda's smiles, liked the perfume that smelled just like what Mama used to wear.

Brenda stopped drinking and continued. "But the judge says he wants to keep custody of you in this county. So I'll still be seeing you." Brenda reached across the car to stroke Ophelia's hair.

On Ophelia's map, there was a red number one written in Harper County to mark her first foster home, not such a bad place except that she had been made to share a room with two other girls. If a girl shared your room, Ophelia discovered, she thought she had a right to ask you questions.

"Where does your mama live?"

"Do you have a daddy?"

"Why did they take you away?"

"What's wrong? The cat got your tongue?"

"If you don't tell us, we'll just ask Madge," said the older one.

That last comment bothered Ophelia, but she didn't think Madge would tell. Ophelia liked the foster mother more than she had expected to, partly because she had not insisted upon being called "Mother."

After a couple of weeks the girls had quit questioning Ophelia, who always kept her head down when she had to be in the room with them. Then one night just as she was dressing for bed it started again.

"How does it feel to be related to someone like your brother?" The older one sang out her question from her bed across the room.

Ophelia said nothing, but she whirled to look at the girl. How did she know Ophelia had a brother?

"Bang, bang." The younger one sat up in the bed she shared with Ophelia and pointed her finger like a gun. "Bang, bang," she said again, and both girls began to laugh.

Ophelia never learned how they found out. Maybe Madge had told them after all. Anyway, it did not matter how they had learned. They knew, and very soon so did everyone else.

"Hey, look," said a boy she passed in the hall. "She's got blood on her shoes."

Ophelia did not cry; did not even slow down. She lowered her head and moved on through the other kids, some laughing, some looking sorry. Inside she raged against both kinds, the laugher and the sympathizer, but she kept her lips pressed shut.

During a spelling test, the girl behind her leaned close and whispered, "How do you spell *murder*?"

Ophelia hunkered low over her paper. When the lunch bell rang, Ophelia did not go to the cafeteria with the others. Instead, she marched into the school office. "I need to use the phone." She tried to make her words sound strong and determined. *Maybe*, she thought, *the secretary will be afraid of me.*

"Students aren't allowed to use the phone," said the woman.

"I have to use the phone." Ophelia crossed her arms and stared straight into the secretary's eyes.

"Just a minute." The secretary stepped back toward the principal's inner office. When she came out she motioned toward the phone behind the counter. "Come on back," she said. "Mrs. James says it's okay."

Ophelia had never used Brenda Phillips's number before, but having it memorized gave her a sense of security. She dialed the number quickly, the secretary watching as if Ophelia might damage the phone.

She recognized the voice even before Brenda identified herself. "It's me, Ophelia," she said. "I'm at school, but I can't stay here. I can't. Will you come to get me now?"

Sitting on a blue chair, Ophelia put back her head to count ceiling tiles. Counting was a habit she had acquired during the waiting she had done lately: count the benches in the courtroom, count the men wearing suits, count the women with gray hair. She heard the secretary's voice, but lost in numbers, she did not realize the woman spoke to her.

This time the voice was loud and very close to Ophelia. "I said a parent has to check you out of school. Were you talking to one of your parents just now?" Hands on her hips, the woman leaned over Ophelia, who slowly changed the position of her head.

Now she looked at the floor. There were squares in the carpet, and Ophelia wanted to count them, wanted to forget the woman and her voice and count to herself.

"Answer me when I ask you a question," said the secretary.

Ophelia crossed her arms over her chest. "No, I did not call my parents. I called my social worker. I can't call my parents because they are both dead. Their blood ran all over our kitchen floor."

The principal came then from her office and said something to the secretary. Ophelia did not hear what the principal said. She began to count the squares in the carpet, and she counted the squares over and over until Brenda Phillips came.

There were thirty-eight squares on her side of the office counter. Ophelia never forgot the number, but she tried hard to forget that first foster home and the first school.

And so Ophelia was moved to Woods, the county that she later marked in red as number two on her map.

"You might not be here long," Brenda told Ophelia when they stopped in front of the small white house that was to be her second foster home.

Had Grandma changed her mind? Had Grandma decided to take her in after all? Ophelia's heart began to beat fast, but she kept her voice calm. "How come?"

Brenda reached out to brush Ophelia's hair from her eyes. "We might find you a new mother and father. Would that be something you would like?"

Ophelia stared wordlessly at the woman. How could she ever have another mother and father?

"Remember how we talked about the three kinds of families—natural, foster, and adopted? How would you feel about being adopted?"

So Ophelia had moved into that second foster home, thinking it might be her last one. Brenda had explained that in early June, just a few weeks away, there would be a big party. Kids who needed homes would be brought by their social workers. People who wanted to adopt would be there, too, along with lots of food, games, and prizes.

"What the heck," Brenda had said just before she left Ophelia. "Even if we don't find you a family, you and I can have a nice day together, right?" She had hugged Ophelia, who breathed in deeply to pull in the smell of Brenda's perfume, Mama's perfume.

Ophelia did not like the new foster mother or her husband. They were stone-faced people who seemed to be angry at each other all the time and at Ophelia when they noticed that she was in the room. She did like the fact that no other children were in the home.

"Besides," she told herself often, "you might not be here long. You might get a new family after the party."

Brenda bought Ophelia a beautiful sundress—white with yellow flowers, tiny straps—and a cute little jacket. The night before the party, Ophelia decided to give her hair a hundred strokes with the hairbrush. Mama always talked about Ophelia's wonderful hair—"like strands of golden silk," she would say as she brushed it. The party would be at a park. Ophelia decided she would try to sit in the sun. Mama always said Ophelia's hair sparkled in the sunlight.

She had just finished the brushing when her foster mother called. " 'Phelia, phone for you."

Ophelia hated the way the woman always left the O off her name, but busy wondering about the phone call, she did not make a face this time. No one ever called her. Her hand shook as she took the phone.

"Hello, honey," said Brenda Phillips. "I'm afraid I've got some sort of bad news for you."

Ophelia was used to bad news. She kept her voice calm. "What? What bad news?"

"I can't take you to the party," Brenda told her. "You'll get to go," she added quickly, "but I can't take you. In fact, I can't be your social worker anymore."

For a second Ophelia thought she might cry, but the tears did not slip from her eyes. "Why not?"

"I just found out I'm going to have a baby, but the

thing is, I'm having trouble. I have to stay in bed for a long time, or I might lose the baby. I might anyway, but I really hope not."

"Oh," said Ophelia. Brenda went on to talk about how Ophelia would really like the new worker and about what time the woman would pick her up. Ophelia hardly listened. She thought about Brenda's perfume and how it smelled just like Mama's.

The woman who came for her early the next day was kind. She smiled at Ophelia, but she did not hug her. Nor did she wear perfume. The trip to the state park took three hours.

"I hope it doesn't rain," the worker said, and she pushed buttons on the car radio, looking for a weather forecast. "Don't worry, though. There's a big lodge. The party will be in there if it's rainy."

Ophelia said nothing. She sat quietly on her side of the seat. For a while she counted trees, but when the countryside changed, trees became too plentiful to count. Ophelia switched to bridges and horses.

It did rain. There would be no sunlight on her hair. Ophelia ate her hot dog and ice cream, but she refused to throw the balls at the wooden targets or to play musical chairs. She sat, shoulders hunched and eyes down, while all around her younger children jumped and ran.

None of the parents came over to talk to Ophelia. *There won't ever be a new family for me*, she thought. She shook her head without even thinking about her hair. She didn't want a new family anyway. No one wanted her, and she did not care, would never hope again.

"Can we leave now?" she asked the social worker before the party was over.

The social worker did not even try to talk Ophelia into staying. On the way out of the lodge, they saw a cute little foster girl walking between a young couple who held her hands. The couple smiled down at the child adoringly.

"Good luck," the social worker said to the couple.

Ophelia looked away from the happy couple. On the way home, she did not even have the energy to count.

4.

‿

When Ophelia set out the second time to read to Miss McKay, she knew she would leave the road and go to the rock for just a little while. She would sit beside the river, and she would think of two things. She would remember the way the other Ophelia died, and she would wonder about the date carved into the rock.

The breeze off the water felt cool. Ophelia lifted her hair away from her face, turning her head from side to side in order to get the full effect of the air. She wished she had worn shorts and a sleeveless shirt so that more of her skin could be touched by the nice wind. She bent low, studying the water, but before long she pulled herself up to leave. Portia McKay did not seem like a woman who would tolerate tardiness.

Miss McKay sat waiting on the porch, but she did not glance up as Ophelia approached. *Probably she doesn't know I'm here*, the girl thought, and she was about to call out a greeting when the woman spoke and slapped at her own shoulder.

"Dang mosquitoes. They'll be gone directly. It's the only good thing about winter." She stood and, without saying anything more, led the way into the house.

Miss McKay took the orange book from the shelf again and motioned for Ophelia to sit again on the couch near the lamp. *Lina would have looked like this girl*, Portia McKay thought. *She would have sat there beside that same lamp, and she might have read from that same book.*

"You look nice in that red blouse," Portia said. "My sister had a red dress, and she looked especially pretty in it, too. I guess blondes always do. Anyway, she had on that dress when I saw her the last time. She was seventeen years old."

"What happened? Why didn't you ever see her again after that day?" Ophelia knew she broke her own rule about never asking personal questions, but the sadness in Miss McKay's voice made the girl wonder.

"She died in childbirth, but what kept me from seeing her was something my father did. It was his fault I never saw her again."

Ophelia followed the woman's gaze to the portrait. "That sounds awful mean," she said.

"Seth McKay was very possibly the meanest man who ever lived." Miss McKay shook her head and gave a small laugh. "No, to be fair I'd have to change that to the meanest man who ever lived in this country. I'll have to admit Adolf Hitler might have been meaner, but let's not waste our reading time talking about Seth McKay. *Hamlet* waits."

After the girl had read for almost an hour, Portia McKay held out her hand. "Enough Shakespeare. I made plum cake."

Ophelia glanced up from the book. She had not planned to stay for even a minute after the reading stopped.

Miss McKay did not wait for an answer, and Ophelia followed her to the kitchen. "See that dish? It belonged to my grandmother. She pointed to the white china cake stand that held the brown plum dessert. "My mother's sister came to see us, just once when I was about seven, and she told me that the cake plate belonged to my grandmother." She shrugged her shoulders. "Seems strange to me sometimes. My grandmother died in 1875, more than 120 years ago, but here's this plate. My grandmother used this plate. She made cakes and put them on this stand with her own hands. I never saw my grandmother, but I'm still using this cake plate."

The woman stared out through the window, as if she had not been talking to the girl at all, as if she did not even know Ophelia stood beside her.

Get out of here, Ophelia thought. *This old lady doesn't pay you to stand around while she mutters to herself about dishes.* She looked toward the kitchen door. Should she go out that way or back through the front room?

"Sit down." Miss McKay pointed toward the kitchen table. Ophelia looked once more at the door, but she sat down. "You go to school over to town, I guess."

Ophelia nodded her head.

"What do you think of living with the Reynoldses?"

Ophelia studied her shoes. *Look, lady*, she thought, *I've been quizzed by experts.* "Do you have friends, dear?" "How do you feel when the other children talk about their parents?" "What kind of dreams do you have?" Sometimes when she felt like it, Ophelia would answer questions, but most of the time she folded her arms and waited.

"Well?" said the woman. "Tell me."

Ophelia didn't want to answer, but she felt her mouth opening. "It's okay, I guess. They're pretty nice to me. I've been in worse places."

Miss McKay nodded her head, and Ophelia felt as if the woman understood those other places, those terrible foster homes.

"What do you think of the school here?"

"It's okay. My science class is really interesting. I don't usually like science, but this teacher makes it lots better."

"Other kids nice to you, are they?" Miss McKay set a plate with cake on the table.

"They leave me alone. That's what I like, being left alone." Ophelia took the fork that Miss McKay held out to her.

"You like to be left alone, do you? That's what I wanted, child. For more than seventy years that's what I wanted. Got it, too. The world's mostly willing to leave a body alone, I guess."

"Not kids in some schools, not when they find out a person's had troubles."

Ophelia took a bite of her cake, and Portia waited until she had time to swallow before she asked, "What kind of troubles?"

The girl looked straight at the woman, and for the first time ever she did not mind answering, "Killing. Bad killing."

The woman left her place beside the cabinet, walked to the table, and sat down across from the girl. "Killing," she repeated softly. "I'm sorry I made you tell me."

"It's okay." Ophelia meant what she said, but she also wanted to change the subject. "I went to the river," she said. Ophelia noticed the change of expression on the woman's face.

"So you saw the rock." Portia pressed her lips together tightly.

"I saw the date, too. Do you know what it means—July 19, 1921?"

"The date?" Portia McKay closed her eyes for a minute and sighed. "The answer, child, is yes and no. I carved that date there myself. On July 19, 1921, I wrote those numbers on that rock. Do I know what it means? I'm not so sure. I've spent more than seventy years trying to decide, but, no, I can't really say I understand what it means."

Miss McKay stood, and Ophelia followed her to the front door. Neither of them said good-bye.

On the way back to the foster home, Ophelia did not

go back to the rock, but she stood for a long time near the trail that led to the water's edge. She stood absolutely still and listened to the roar of the water.

Finally, she made herself begin to walk. Mrs. Reynolds might complain if she had to stay up past her bedtime waiting for her to get home. Ophelia did not want to upset Mrs. Reynolds. It was true that things were working well. This was not a bad foster home. No one bothered her at school. Best of all was the twenty-dollar bill Miss McKay had put in her hand just as she left.

"I haven't finished the book yet," Ophelia had protested, but Miss McKay shook her head.

Twenty dollars. Ophelia squeezed the bill. Now she had thirty-five dollars. Soon she would have the seventy-five needed for her ticket home. She knew she couldn't stay in Deer Run, but she wanted to go there just once more. She wanted to see the house again, and she wanted to go to the cemetery to see the graves.

Would they let her go? Probably not alone. She didn't want to go home with a social worker, but she might have to have someone with her. Ophelia smiled. When the time came, she might ask Miss McKay to go with her, and Ophelia felt certain the woman would be willing.

Mr. and Mrs. Reynolds were watching the evening

news when Ophelia came in, but Mrs. Reynolds followed her to her room. "I don't know as it's a good idea, you being out in the dark like this."

Ophelia's heart began to race. Evenings were getting short, not enough time before dark for supper and spending any real time at Miss McKay's. She took a deep breath and leaned against the wall before she spoke. Her voice needed to be just right, insistent without an arguing tone. "It's not far. I'm not afraid. No one's out much on this road after dark."

Mrs. Reynolds stood in the doorway, her body filling the opening. "My other girls went mostly on Saturdays and Sundays when the days started getting short." She wrinkled her forehead.

"I really like Miss McKay," Ophelia said. "I think she likes me, too."

Mrs. Reynolds laughed. "Well, bless your heart. I don't know as I've ever heard a single soul say they liked Portia McKay, and if she likes you, that's sure enough a first."

"Can I keep going, then?" Ophelia held her breath.

"Yes, sweetheart. You just keep right on going. My mama always did say there ain't nothing in the dark that ain't there in the daylight."

5.

When her foster mother left the room, Ophelia went to the bureau to take out the small atlas. Back on the bed, she opened it to the Oklahoma page. There it was, the red dot on the spot Deer Run occupied. "I'm coming home, Mama," she whispered. "I'll see you soon, Mama." She paused to bite at her lip, then she added, "You too, Daddy. I'll see you too."

For a long time after that terrible day, Ophelia had been angry with her father, too angry to mourn his death. Looking at the family picture Grandma had let her keep, she would kiss the face of her mother and of Roy, but she would point at her father and say, "You caused this. It's all your fault." Once she had taken a pair of scissors with the intention of cutting her father from the picture, but she had too much trouble getting the picture from its big wooden frame.

Now she had forgiven her father, almost. She had loved Daddy. Hadn't he always been good to her, bringing her little gifts when he came home from a sales trip, letting her take the chewing gum from his coat pocket? He had been good to Roy, too, in the happy early days.

She remembered one Saturday when Roy was ten and she was five. It was June, not long before Father's Day. Daddy had been pitching balls to Roy in the backyard, but Daddy came in to make some business phone calls.

"Come on out to the kitchen," Roy told Ophelia, and she put down her doll to follow her big brother.

Roy sat down at the kitchen table and pointed Ophelia toward a chair. "We've got to have a business meeting," he told her.

"Like Daddy does?"

Roy nodded his head. "In one week it will be Father's Day. Do you know what that means?"

Ophelia didn't, not exactly, but she said, "Yes."

"Well, we got to get Daddy a gift," Roy told her. "Do you have any money?"

"Yes," Ophelia said again. "I have lots of money in my room. Grandma gave it to me."

"Good. Go get it."

Ophelia remembered coming back, coins clutched in her hand. "See!" She spread them on the table, a quarter, two dimes, and two nickels.

Roy sighed. "Fifty-five cents. That won't buy much."

"Well," said Ophelia, but she couldn't think of anything to add.

"We just got to make some money." Roy jumped up from his chair. "Hey! I've got an idea. We'll sell lemonade!"

Mama made a big pitcher of lemonade. Roy carried out his chair and then came back to help Ophelia, who had been dragging hers. "Now we need a table," he said. "There's a pile of boards in the garage."

Roy and Ophelia worked at nailing boards, but the legs wouldn't hold up the top. Daddy came out of the back door. "What are you trying to make?" he asked.

"A table for our lemonade," Roy said.

"We're going to make money to buy a present for Father's Day," said Ophelia.

"Ophelia!" Roy yelled. "It's supposed to be a surprise."

Daddy laughed. "Well, nobody said who the present is for."

Daddy helped build the table, and he bought the last

two glasses of lemonade for himself and Mama, but before the last two glasses, a man from the newspaper came and took Roy and Ophelia's picture.

Ophelia could remember the picture, with the headline "Summer Business" beneath it. She remembered Roy's face, round and smiling, and her own face turned toward the big brother she loved. Most of all she remembered the tie they bought and how Daddy had worn it every day for a very long time.

Now Ophelia sat on the bed in her foster home and wondered what had gone wrong between Roy and Daddy. A day came to her mind, a day Mama and Daddy had argued in the living room about Roy.

"Just show him you care about him, Joe," Mama had yelled. Her voice dropped some, but still Ophelia could hear from the dining room where she had her homework on the table. "I worry about Roy. He needs you so much. Can't you see that?"

"You think so? He won't even toss a ball around with me anymore!" Ophelia heard Daddy stomp over to the rocking chair, and she heard the squeak as he began to rock.

"Roy has never really been interested in playing ball. He did enjoy doing it with you." Mama paused. "He enjoyed it until you got too rough on him. Joe, you're so uptight and angry, and you take it out on Roy."

The rocking stopped, and Daddy's feet made pacing noises on the hardwood floors. "And you coddle him, Sylvia. It's got to stop. Roy needs to grow up!"

"Sweetheart, listen to how angry you are," Mama said. "Maybe you should see a doctor. They have medicine that can help a person calm down."

"Good Lord," Daddy yelled. "I'm not some middle-aged woman going through menopause. Get off my back." Daddy turned on the TV, loud.

Mama came into the dining room. Ophelia saw the tears in her eyes, but she wanted to ask Mama a question. "What's menopause?"

Mama walked over to put her arm on Ophelia's shoulder. "It's something you don't have to worry about for a long, long time," she said. "And you don't have to worry about Roy or Daddy, either."

Mama went on into the kitchen. Ophelia sat still in her chair, thinking about what Mama and Daddy had said. Who was right? She knew that sometimes Mama and Roy kept secrets from Daddy, like bad grades and how sometimes Mama cleaned Roy's room and let Daddy think Roy had done it.

The next day, though, Ophelia knew for sure that Daddy was wrong. She and Roy were in the family room, Ophelia at the little puzzle table they kept in the corner, working on a Statue of Liberty puzzle. Roy played a jazz song on his trumpet, but he must have watched Ophelia, too, because he stopped playing and came to help when she spent a long time looking for a piece for the torch.

"Here," he said after a minute. "This is the piece of the lamp you need." For a while they worked together on the puzzle. Then Roy drifted back to the couch and his music.

Things were great until Daddy came in. "Stop blasting on that damn horn," he yelled. "All you care about is that horn and marching up and down on the football field at halftime when you should be playing ball."

"What have you got against the band?" Roy's face was red.

"I don't have anything against the band except maybe that prissy majorette or whatever they call him."

"Drum major, Dad. That's what Erick is, and you know he's my friend. Why can't you just lay off him?" Roy put the horn back to his lips.

"Stop it!" Daddy yanked Roy's trumpet from his hands and threw it on the floor.

"Don't, Dad! Please!" Roy jumped up and pulled on Daddy's arm, but Daddy shoved him off and stomped his foot on the horn hard.

Roy sank onto the couch, his hands over his face. Ophelia ran to pick up the horn. It was bent pretty badly, but she thought it could be straightened out.

"Get up from that couch," Daddy thundered. "I just saw some boys about your age playing basketball over at the park. Go over there and play with them."

"Dad," said Roy in a hopeless tone. "Those boys don't want to play with me. I'm way too little for basketball. Besides, they don't even like me."

Ophelia could see that Daddy was calmer now. He wiped the sweat from his forehead with his shirtsleeve. "How do you know they don't like you? You didn't see them. You don't know who they are."

Roy looked up, and Ophelia could see that he had been crying. "I don't have to know who they are. None of the guys at school like me. None of them would play basketball with me."

Daddy's eyes looked as if they might pop from their sockets. "If that's so, it's because you spend all of your time with that sissy boy. Stop sitting around on Saturday playing music." He reached out and jerked Roy to his feet. "Get out and do something, why don't you?"

Roy pushed Daddy's arm away and ran upstairs to his room. Daddy sank down on the couch where Roy had sat. He put his face in his hands, just the way Roy had.

Ophelia stood quietly, thinking how much Daddy and Roy looked alike and how sad they both were. She started to move silently away, but Daddy's voice stopped her.

"Go upstairs and tell your brother I'll leave a signed check for him on the table. When your mother comes in, I'm sure she'll take him to buy a new horn." Daddy's voice sounded very, very tired.

Portia McKay cut a slice of plum cake for herself. She had sat without eating while the girl ate hers. Poor thing. She reminded Portia of a wounded creature, maybe a bird with a broken wing or a rabbit with a leg hurt in a trap. Such a pretty little thing.

She carried her cake to the table and took up her usual study of what lay outside. Darkness had already settled over the hillside. "Comes early these days," she said aloud. The girl had walked home in the dark. Portia wondered if she was afraid. No, Ophelia didn't seem the type who had the luxury of fearing the dark.

The girl had so much hurt inside her. Portia wished she could help. She hadn't wanted to help anyone in a very long time, not since Lina. She had wanted to help Lina, had been desperate to help Lina. And Daniel, poor Daniel.

Portia could remember the spring day she and Lina had first seen Daniel.

Blackberries covered the hillsides, and the girls had three pails to fill. "You're eating too many," Lina said, and held out her pickings. "See, my bucket's almost half full." But it was Lina who had her mouth full, juice running down her chin, when Daniel came around the bend on the trail.

"Well, hello." His hand went immediately to remove his black felt hat. His skin was suntanned, and his eyes were the color of warm brown earth.

Portia moved to stand beside her sister and waited for Lina to speak, even though her mouth still held berries.

"Don't I even get a how-do?" The young man smiled, and the smile changed his eyes as if a light had been added behind them.

"Her mouth's full," said Portia quietly.

"Now it isn't, but I don't know as I intend to say hello to the likes of you." Lina put her hand over her mouth to wipe at the juice, but Portia could see the smile. Lina intended to talk to this fellow. Portia edged away from Lina to get a better view of the trail. Father had strict rules about talking to boys.

"My name's Daniel. Daniel Dunlap. I reckon you're the McKay girls. I work at your daddy's mill, cutting trees. Foreman Peters warned us mill boys right off to stay away from the McKay girls."

"But you're talking to us, aren't you?" Lina took off her sunbonnet. Portia watched Daniel's eyes as Lina's golden hair came tumbling down to settle in long shining curls around her face.

He's looking at her like she's a piece of candy, Portia thought, and her heart began to beat faster. Just last week Lina had said, "Other girls have beaus and go to dances." She pulled a chair over to settle in front of the dresser mirror.

"Other girls don't live with Father," said Portia, "and you know what he'll do if he catches you staring into that mirror again."

"I thought sure he'd bust it last time." Lina shrugged her shoulders. "Father doesn't own us, Porty."

Portia pulled the spread across the bed she was making. "He doesn't? Where did you get that idea?"

"He doesn't own me. I'm seventeen years old, and I

intend to have a fellow," Lina said, but she got up from in front of the mirror and scooted the chair away.

Now here was Lina making eyes at this Daniel right where Father could come through the pines or around the curve in the trail at any minute.

"We'd better go." Portia tugged at her sister's arm, but Lina did not budge.

Daniel Dunlap picked up Portia's pail. "Why, you don't have even half a bucket yet. You can't quit now. I expect your pa is partial to berry cobbler."

"Goodness no. There's no reason for us to quit." Lina turned to the bush and put out her hand for a berry, but she looked back over her shoulder to smile at Daniel. "You best be getting on your way, Mr. Daniel Dunlap, else that foreman you mentioned is likely to be coming after you."

"On my own time. I'm off at two. Ain't no one going to be looking for me." He moved to stand beside Lina. "Don't see why I shouldn't help a couple of ladies pick berries."

For almost an hour they picked, Daniel and Lina smiling at each other, Portia glancing furtively over her shoulder toward the trail. It had always been her habit to poke about with a long stick before moving to a new bush. Now Portia forgot to watch for rattlesnakes.

"We'll be here again tomorrow," Lina said after finally agreeing with Portia that it was time to go home.

"Could be I'll be coming this way," Daniel said with a grin.

"Could be I'll speak to you." Lina turned away from him with a toss of her head to make her hair move in the sun. The girls had made only a few steps when Lina called out, "Good-bye, Mr. Daniel Dunlap."

"Good-bye, fair ladies," Daniel shouted. His voice seemed to bounce from the pines. Both girls turned to watch him disappear around the curve. Lina stood smiling, but there was no smile on her sister's face.

"We can't go back there," said Portia. "We can't ever see that fellow again. You know we can't."

Lina did not even stop smiling. "I don't know what you're going to do," she said, "but I intend to be picking berries right here on this hillside tomorrow." She stopped walking and put her hand on Portia's arm. "Oh, don't be such a worrywart, Porty. What harm can there be in a little berry picking?"

After supper that night, Father complimented the food. "Fine gravy," he said, "and I never tasted better berry cobbler. This year's crop must be extra good." He pushed back his chair and reached for his pipe. "You girls be sure to get enough of those berries to put up plenty of jars against winter. God gives us those berries. It'd be a downright sin not to take advantage of them."

Lina, who had already begun to clear the table, reached for her father's plate and smiled over his head at Portia. "I said just practically the same thing to Portia this very afternoon. I said, 'It would be just a sin not to go out tomorrow and enjoy gathering what God has given us to enjoy.'"

"I'm not going," Portia told her sister when they were in bed that night. "If you want to meet some silly mill hand, you go right ahead, but you'll sure enough have to go by yourself. I'm not risking a beating for such nonsense." She turned on her side away from her sister.

"Do as you please. It's no matter to me." Lina, too, threw herself over on her side.

For a long time the girls lay quietly. Far off in the distance a bobcat cried, and from the tree near the window, a night bird called. Portia listened for the even breathing that would tell her Lina slept, but she heard only a sigh. "I'll go with you," she muttered at last. "I'm against it, but if you go I might as well go, too. Father would probably beat me anyway for not telling him."

"I'm glad," Lina said. "Awful glad. I'd have gone

even without you. I'd sure have been afraid, but, Portia, nothing could keep me from seeing Daniel Dunlap again. I like him. I really, really like him."

Long after Lina began to breathe the even breaths of sleep, Portia lay awake, listening to the sounds of night.

That spring, the one Portia remembered as the last spring of her childhood, the berries seemed to last longer than any other spring. Each afternoon they picked, always with the help of Daniel Dunlap, and always Portia took her pail a few feet away. She liked to put bushes between herself and the other two pickers. On the third day of picking before she got away, she saw them exchange a kiss. Daniel leaned down to brush his lips across Lina's.

It was a quick, innocent kiss, but still a kiss, and enough to make Portia cold with fear despite the warm afternoon sun. She was still worrying about the kiss when she heard the cat.

She closed her eyes to listen hard. There it was again, a pitiful little cry from a tall cottonwood tree. A small yellow cat clung precariously to a high branch.

"It's a kitten," Portia yelled, and Lina came running with Daniel following.

"Oh," said Lina, "poor thing. It's scared to death."

Daniel took off his hat and shaded his eyes to look

up at the kitten. "Reckon it'll be all right," he said. "Cat's have a way of getting out of scrapes pretty good."

"We can't just leave the poor thing up there." Lina put her hand on Daniel's arm and leaned toward him.

"It's pretty far up," Daniel said, "and there aren't any branches low down. It'd be pretty hard to get it down."

Lina stepped away from Daniel. "Well," she said, "I'm going to get it." She turned to Portia. "You'll help me, won't you, Porty?"

Before Portia could speak, Daniel said, "Whoa, now. I never said I wasn't willing to go up and get it. I'll figure out a way."

The way involved the girls boosting Daniel, one pushing on each leg wrapped around the tree. "Just a little more," he said, and he used his hands to clutch at the trunk. Finally he was able to grab on to the lowest branch, swing his legs up, and raise his body.

Both girls, exhausted, leaned against the tree trunk, but Lina clapped for Daniel. "Oh, I knew you'd be able to do it," she said.

Daniel looked at the cat far above his head. "Well," he drawled, "I haven't exactly done it yet."

The girls watched while Daniel moved up toward the cat. "Isn't he wonderful?" Lina whispered.

Anna Myers

Portia didn't see what was so wonderful about climbing a tree, but when Daniel got his hand on the cat what happened did make her like Daniel. "Dang thing bit me," he yelled, and Portia thought he would drop the kitten. Instead he held the kitten close, stroked it, and spoke softly to the yellow ball of fur.

"He's not like Father," Lina whispered, "not at all."

Daniel scratched his chin. "Well," he said, "now I've got to get down from here using one hand. Wish I had a big pocket to stick this fellow in."

"Oh, Daniel, be awful careful." Lina's face looked worried.

"Oh, don't worry. I won't get myself hurt none," he called down.

He moved carefully down the tree and lowered himself from the last branch, then dropped the last few feet.

Lina three her arms around him, and the kiss she gave him was not a quick brush of the lips. Portia turned away.

When she looked back, Lina had the kitten. "You're not planning to take that cat home!"

Lina shook her curls. "I most certainly am. Oh, don't worry, Porty. We'll tell Father it just wandered up."

"Have you forgotten Tom?" Portia asked.

62

"Don't worry," Lina repeated, but Portia did worry. On the way home, it was Portia who carried the kitten. Daniel and Lina walked in front of her, their arms intertwined.

"We're getting close," Portia called. Lina and Daniel stopped walking, but they looked only at each other. Daniel made no move toward leaving.

Portia walked to Lina and pulled at her arm. "We'd better hurry. It's time we started Father's supper."

Lina did not budge. Her eyes seemed fastened to Daniel's. "You go on, Porty," she said. "I'll be along."

Portia, carrying the kitten, walked slowly through the trees. She sat down on a big rock to wait for her sister. Finally, Lina came, her face red and her eyes shining. "I love him, Porty," she said. "You're only thirteen, so you don't understand. But when he touches me, I just tingle all over."

Portia turned her head away. "Father's supper can't wait for tingling," she muttered.

Lina reached for the kitten. "Let me carry it," she said. "Oh, what a sweet thing. We'll call it Sunshine. That could be for a boy or a girl.

The girls had had a gray cat that had been given to them as a tiny kitten two years earlier. Father had declared it to be a male and named it Tom.

Father didn't object to the cat because there were mice in the barn. He didn't object until one day when he and the girls came home from a trip to town.

Taking the harness from the horse, Father walked to hang it on its place on the wall. "The cat!" he yelled, and bent to look under the feed trough. The girls hurried to see. Tom lay under the trough with four kittens!

"Oh, look!" Portia put out her hand to touch a kitten, but Father slapped her hand.

"Stand back," he ordered.

With a swoop he jerked Tom up and banged the cat's gray head hard against the rock foundation of the feed trough.

"No," shrieked Portia, but Lina put her hand across her sister's mouth and pulled her toward the barn door.

He killed the kittens two at a time.

Crying, the girls ran toward the house. At the back steps Portia stopped, overwhelmed with sickness. She vomited into the grass, then leaned against the porch rail.

Lina pulled her handkerchief from her skirt pocket and wiped Portia's face.

"He didn't have to kill them," Portia said. "There are lots of mice in the barn."

"Oh," said Lina, "don't you understand? Father

didn't kill them because they would need to be fed. He killed them because Tom defied him. Tom had the nerve to go against Father and be a female."

Remembering the cat, Portia turned back to study her sister's face. How could Lina be so happy? Didn't she know what lay ahead?

They picked lots of berries that summer, but berries do not last long. When the berries were gone, so was the excuse for being away from home in the afternoon. The sawmill stood right beside the house, and with their father going in and out, the girls had to be always at their chores.

Daniel Dunlap took chances, hiding in the barn until Lina came out to do the evening milking, sneaking into the back door once in broad daylight with Father right there on the front porch.

Portia, always lifting a curtain's edge to watch for father, begged both Lina and Daniel to stop the danger-ous behavior. "Don't worry, little girl." Daniel would smile the big slow smile that spread from his mouth and eyes to take in his entire face. "I'm a lucky man. Why, if God hadn't meant us to be together, I wouldn't have been lucky enough to come down that trail and find me two angels picking berries."

Lina, too much in love to think of anything except

Daniel, refused to listen to Portia's fears either. "I won't have to wear these awful lace-up shoes much longer," she said one morning as the girls dressed.

"Oh? Don't imagine Father will change his mind about the kind of shoes we order from the catalogue."

Lina finished tying her shoes and began to whirl about the room, her plaid shirt standing out in the morning breeze. "Father won't be choosing my shoes for me, not for long. I wasn't going to tell you till we knew when, but I'm too happy to keep it a secret." She danced over to stop in front of the bed where Portia sat.

"What? What secret?" Portia had trouble moving her lips.

"I'm getting married! Just as soon as Daniel has saved up a little more money!"

Portia spoke only one word: "Father."

"Daniel will hide his wagon in the woods. We'll wait for a chance." Lina reached out to touch her sister's face. "Oh, Porty, don't look so sad. You'll go with us, of course!"

Portia felt tears come to her eyes and roll down her cheeks. "Daniel said that? He said I could come?"

Lina sat beside Portia and put her arm across her sister's shoulder. "Of course, silly. You didn't think I'd ever go off and leave you, did you?"

Portia shook her head no, but she had. The fear of Lina's leaving had been almost as strong as the fear that her father might discover Lina and Daniel together.

She would go away with Lina and Daniel! Portia jumped from the bed and pulled Lina with her. The two girls began to twirl about the room. Portia felt so light, she thought she might begin to float.

The lightness lasted only as long as the morning. That afternoon what Portia had feared happened. Lina came running into the house. "Father caught me with Daniel," she shrieked, her eyes wild with fear. "He's using the whip on him."

Portia, her hands dripping with dishwater, rushed toward the window. Lina reached out to grab her sister's arm. "You can't see anything. They're in the barn. Father will kill him. Oh, Portia, he will."

The girls stayed, shaking, by the window. With the whip still in his hand, Father came out of the barn. "Peters!" The shout came clearly through the window, and they watched the sawmill foreman run to their father, who gestured toward the barn, then headed toward the house.

"He's coming!" Almost before Portia could put her arm around her sister, he thundered into the room.

To Portia, Father always seemed even taller when he

was angry. His wide-brimmed straw hat was in one hand. His other arm shot out, the fingers closed tightly around Lina's wrist.

With one quick jerk, he pulled Lina away from her sister. Then Portia saw him open his massive fist, and she closed her eyes. The quick thwacking sound of Father's hand across Lina's face seemed to force Portia's eyes open to see Lina falling backward.

In a second she was beside her sister on the floor, lifting her head. The puffy red print of her father's palm covered Lina's cheek. Seth McKay towered above the girls. "Get up," he said. "And get to your chores, both of you. I want no talk between you of that good-for-nothing." He gestured with his arm toward the barn. "I've told Peters to haul him to town. I've also told Peters to make sure he knows I'll kill him if he ever sets foot on my place again."

He turned and stomped away. "He was warned," he said just before he slammed out the kitchen door. "All the sawmill hands are warned never to touch one of my girls."

Lina jumped up and ran back to the window. "Don't," Portia yelled, but Lina pushed the curtain back.

"Oh," she gasped. "He's bloody, all bloody."

"Come away from the window." Portia pulled at her sister's arm. "Father might see you."

Lina shook her head, and Portia, too, looked out. Peters had brought a wagon to the barn. Two men lifted Daniel's body to put it in the back. His clothes hung in shreds and blood streamed from great open gashes.

By the next morning, Sunday, Lina's face was purple and swollen. Portia fixed her father's usual breakfast of pancakes. "We'll have prayers in the parlor," he said when he had eaten the last bite.

And so they gathered, the three of them. Seth McKay sat in his rocking chair, his great black Bible open across his lap.

The girls knelt beside the settee. First he read from Psalms, and then in a loud voice he began to pray. "Oh, Lord, please forgive thy wayward child, Carolina, and cleanse her sinner's soul." His voice went on and on. Portia opened one eye just enough to peek at Lina, whose head was bowed, tears squeezed out from the tightly closed lids. Portia felt certain that the tears were not tears of repentance. They were for Daniel, for the loss of him and for his wounds.

6.

⌒

Ophelia felt uncomfortable around the boy who sat in front of her in English and history. Both teachers seated kids according to the alphabet, and Mark Haines had the desk in front of her for two periods. When Ophelia came in to either class, she could expect to find Mark's long legs and big feet sticking out in the aisle as if he owned it.

But it was more than the feet that bothered Ophelia. For five years, she had worked hard at making no real connection with the kids around her. Mark would not be ignored. He always grinned at Ophelia, who kept her eyes down and ignored the stream of jokes and wisecracks he kept going for the amusement of the other kids.

The thing that troubled Ophelia most was that she

did not want to ignore Mark. When he smiled at her, the corners of her mouth tried to turn up. She fought to keep them down. She wished she could sit on the other side of the room.

On a day in October, he seemed quieter than usual. He was turned in his seat so that he watched Ophelia settle into her chair. "Ophelia Holloway?" He leaned his elbow on her desk. "Your name sounds so familiar to me."

Ophelia looked down at her English book and wished he would turn back around. Mark wrinkled his forehead. "Why's your name so familiar?"

"Ophelia's a character from *Hamlet*." She hoped he would turn around now. Why wasn't the bell ringing? Didn't they keep the bells on schedule in this school?

"Hamlet? Is that in Oklahoma?"

"*Hamlet* is a play written by William Shakespeare." She made no attempt to hide her exasperation.

"Hey, it was a joke. Okay? No need to get so bent out of shape. Where you from, anyway?"

Ophelia squirmed in her seat. Why didn't this boy just turn around and leave her alone? She should show him again that she felt irritated, but his smile got to her. "Oh, I've lived lots of places." She looked down again.

"Well, I'm glad you're here now." Just then the bell

rang, and the teacher came in. "Here comes the witch," Mark whispered, and he turned around.

Ophelia did not listen to anything Miss Talley said. Instead, she thought about Mark Haines. "That sounds so familiar to me" kept going through her mind. *Mark Haines must remember my name from the news. Maybe he has relatives who live in Deer Run, or maybe he remembers me from the magazine. Was it* Time *or* Newsweek *or some other magazine like that?*

"The whole thing is in this story," the counselor at last year's school had said. She held up the magazine.

"It couldn't tell the whole story," Ophelia corrected her.

"What do you mean?" the counselor had asked.

Ophelia, who had begun to count the books on the counselor's shelf, said nothing. She didn't care about the magazine, not really. Everyone at this school already knew what had happened in her family. Besides, she wouldn't be back here next year. She had acted up enough to make sure of that. After the last time she had flooded the bathroom, her foster mother had told her that she would be moving when school was finished for the summer.

The magazine article hadn't meant much then, but now it did. Ophelia couldn't stand this school if these kids started to talk about what had happened. What if Mark Haines or someone else in this school saw that magazine article now? The social worker had said they wouldn't move her again, no matter what she pulled. She was so tired of her life, tired of living with that terrible night. Maybe she should just give up.

No, she would try once more to make sure her secret didn't get out. If her efforts didn't work, she would never try again, not anything. She would be like that first Ophelia. Before class was over, she knew what she would try, and she put her plan to work at lunchtime.

The school librarian smiled at Ophelia when she came through the door, but Ophelia looked away. She did like Mrs. Burris, who never questioned her about why she spent her lunch periods alone in the library.

Usually Ophelia headed for a table at the back to read unless she needed a new book. She had never really noticed the magazines before, but now she stopped and looked around for them.

Good, there they were—and off in a corner, too! She glanced at Mrs. Burris, who had sat down in her office. *She's probably going to eat her lunch*, thought Ophelia. She found the back issues of the newsmagazines stacked on a shelf beneath the displayed current issue.

Her hand shook as she went through last spring's

stack. There it was, "Kids Who Kill" written across the top. Ophelia glanced over her shoulder. No one could see her. Quickly she slipped the magazine inside her notebook.

She moved, eyes down, toward her usual table, but when she came around the big bookshelf, she stopped and gave a gasp of surprise. Mrs. Burris always kept a puzzle on a small library table. Ophelia had seen girls working on it in the morning, but no one had ever been at the table at lunchtime. Once or twice Ophelia had stopped beside the table, but puzzles made her think of Roy. She had moved on. But now someone sat at the table, a boy, Mark Haines.

For a second Ophelia clutched the notebook with the magazine inside tightly to her chest, as if Mark might try to take it from her.

"Hi." He looked up from the puzzle, and his smile made Ophelia able to relax her grip on the notebook.

No one else was around. "Where are your friends?" She had never seen Mark without a bunch of other kids.

He shrugged his shoulders. "I could say I wanted to be by myself. You know that I'm really the quiet, serious type."

"What do you mean 'could say'?"

"Well, I could say that, but you'd know it was a lie.

You'd know I probably saw you come in and followed you because I wanted to talk to you." He picked up a piece of the puzzle and held it out to her. "You want to help me put together the U.S. capitol?"

Ophelia looked at the piece Mark held out to her, and she looked at her own hand, slowly moving to take the piece. She sat down, but she kept the notebook in her lap.

"Good!"

For a few minutes they worked quietly. Ophelia found several pieces of the dome. "You're good at this," Mark said.

"I used to do puzzles a lot," Ophelia said softly.

"Hey, you're starting to talk to me."

Ophelia, holding her notebook, stood up. "But I've got to go."

"Wait a minute." Mark pushed back his chair too. "I want to ask you something. I've got my driver's license now."

Ophelia took a step backward. "I guess that's pretty nice." She turned then and hurried away, out the library door, down the hall, and into the girls' rest room.

With relief, Ophelia saw that she was alone inside the rest room. She leaned against the wall to get her breath. Mark Haines had been about to ask her for a date. Ophelia felt certain of it, and the idea made her feel shaky. She couldn't do something like going out on a date. Things like that were for normal people, people who did not have hidden magazines with pictures of murdered family members.

She took a deep breath. She would take the magazine home, and she would destroy it. Maybe it was silly to go to all the trouble. Someone in the school was bound to find out sooner or later what Roy had done.

Still, she did not want Mark Haines to be the one. Sometimes she felt it might be best just to announce in each of her classes that her brother was a killer. Of course, she never could tell that the most terrible thing Roy did had been her fault. She would never tell anyone about her guilt. She would take her secret to her grave.

Ophelia kept the magazine in her notebook all afternoon, and her mind stayed glued to the pages. She would take it to her foster home, but before she destroyed it, she would read what had been written about her family. When she got off the yellow bus, she did not go home. Instead she headed for the river.

Rain had fallen all the night before, and the roar of the water reached Ophelia's ears even before she came to the road. The river was powerful, more powerful than the brook the other Ophelia had died in. Maybe she should stay away from the river the way Miss McKay had said, but when she came near the path to the rock, Ophelia left the road.

When she was settled in that special seat on the rock, she opened the magazine to page twenty-three. Roy stared up at her, Roy in a green T-shirt. It was a school picture that Ophelia had never seen. She tried to remember why.

Oh, yes. "I didn't pay for them," Roy had said when Ophelia had brought her pictures home and their mother had asked about Roy's. "I didn't want sixteen pictures of me to stick in some drawer," he had said, and he pretended to be interested in the television program he switched on.

Ophelia sat on the rock and studied the face in the picture. Why didn't Roy have his glasses? Then she remembered Roy's glasses had been broken the night before the picture was taken, the October night Daddy and Roy had argued about the school dance. His glasses were broken during the fight.

They had been at the table. "Guy Frick was telling me yesterday that his son's taking a girl to the dance at the high school tomorrow night." Daddy looked at Roy. "You going to the dance?"

"No." Roy put ketchup on his meat and did not look up. "You know I don't go to dances."

"You have a girl?" Daddy's voice got louder with each word.

"No, Dad. I don't have a girl." Roy started to get up from the table.

"Sit down." Daddy pounded his fist on the table hard enough to shake the plates. "You haven't eaten a bite of that food."

"I don't want it," Roy said quietly.

"You took it out, and you're going to eat it."

Roy sank back in his chair and picked up the spoon.

"Do you ever even talk to girls at school?" Daddy yelled.

"No." Roy took a bite of roast beef.

"You don't even talk to the girls?" Daddy gave Roy a disgusted look. "I suppose you spend all your time talking to that sissy, green-haired Erick."

"Stop it, Joe," Mama screamed, but Roy was up and moving past Daddy's chair toward the door.

Ophelia sat crying at the table, watching Daddy grab Roy's arm and slap his face. When Roy was gone and Daddy had gone back to his food, Ophelia noticed Roy's black-rimmed glasses on the floor. She didn't know whether Daddy had knocked them off and broken them, or whether they had fallen off. Maybe Roy had stepped on them as he ran from the room.

Portia McKay tried to make her grocery list, but her mind kept straying. Sometimes she thought of the girl, Ophelia, and sometimes she thought about cats. A small white cat sat on the window box just outside the kitchen window. The cat had appeared yesterday and had made Portia remember Sunshine.

She left her place at the table, took milk from the refrigerator, and opened the back door. Portia poured milk into the saucer she had put out for the cat.

"Kitty, kitty," she called. The white cat came, but instead of drinking from the saucer, it darted into the kitchen before Portia closed the door.

"Guess you need a friend more than you need food," the woman said, and for a minute she let the kitten rub against her leg. Then she bent, lifted the animal, and put it outside. "I'm too old to be friendly with you," she said.

Portia went back to her task. Making the list, carefully planning her small meals, was a job Portia did not have to do. She had plenty of money, left from the days when the sawmill had been the biggest industry in the county. Portia could well afford to give Bernice Reynolds money and say, "Buy lots of good things," but she planned her list as if money were the issue.

"Habit," she said aloud. She had long ago formed the habit of punishing herself however possible.

Making the list, usually a short task, took all morning, and she had just written down salt, the last item, when Bernice Reynolds knocked at the kitchen door.

"It's warm out there, more like June than October." The large woman's hair was wet with perspiration.

"Sit down." Portia pulled a chair back from the table. "Let me get you a glass of iced tea."

Mrs. Reynolds smiled with surprise. "Well, that'd be real fine."

"Your foster girl reads very nicely." Portia handed the tea to Bernice, who took a drink before she spoke.

"She's a good girl, too, I think." She smiled ruefully. "You can never be sure about one of the fosters. They've been through so much."

"What's this one's story?" Portia had settled herself across the table from Bernice.

"W-e-l-l." Bernice drew out the word while she thought. Usually she did not mind talking about her foster kids despite the fact that she was not supposed to do so. This girl's story, though, was different. She knew Ophelia could suffer if the story got out, but she also knew that Portia McKay had no contact with the people in town. Talking to someone about the girl would be nice, but after all, Portia McKay had never been anxious to talk with her before.

Bernice shook her head. "I'm told not to talk about the kids' pasts," she said, and she put her glass to her mouth for a long drink.

"I certainly wouldn't want you to break any rules." Portia stood up and went to the cabinet for the grocery list. Her eyes went to the window box and the white cat that had settled back there. An idea came to her mind. "A kitten came up to the house," she said, and she made her voice friendly. "I wonder if the girl could have it? You could buy the food with my other groceries."

"She'd have to keep it in her room most of the time and see to the litter box herself," Bernice said.

"She seems like a responsible girl."

Bernice nodded her head. "I could take it home with me when I bring back your things."

"If you don't mind," Portia surprised herself by saying, "I'd like to give it to her myself."

7.

Ophelia did not stay long on the rock. Her family's part of the story was only one page. It took only a short time to read. She stared hard at one sentence and read the words aloud. "When the killing stopped, Ophelia Holloway, who was ten years old at the time, was totally alone." She could hardly hear her own words above the roar of the river.

"Can I skip supper?" Ophelia asked her foster mother when she had made herself leave the rock to go home. "I'd like to go early to Miss McKay's. I'll be back to do the dishes."

Bernice Reynolds paused in her carrot chopping to look at the girl. "Goodness, what's the hurry? None of my other girls ever spent as much time there as you do."

Ophelia ignored the question. "Please," she said.

"Well, I don't know as I care, but I'm going to save you something to eat. Seems to me you're even thinner now than when you came."

Ophelia made herself wait until Mrs. Reynolds finished talking. "Thank you," she said, and she was gone.

The path had become familiar to her, more comfortable than any spot she had known since leaving Deer Run. On other days she had often paused to study the changing colors of the leaves on a post oak tree or to listen to a woodpecker's work in a poplar.

During the last month they had finished *Hamlet* and a novel called *The Razor's Edge*. She liked reading to Miss McKay, who had lent her *Hamlet* when they finished. "I'll take good care of it," Ophelia had promised. "I'd like to study it some."

Now she held the magazine under her arm as she hurried down the rocky road. She might decide to let Miss McKay see that magazine. Her eyes were good enough to read the big headline: "Kids Who Kill." If she saw the headline, she would surely ask questions. It would be a way to get into it all. Ophelia thought she might want to tell Portia McKay the story, might want to hear what the woman would say about what had happened.

When the house came into view, Ophelia saw the

woman at the window. *She's waiting for me*, Ophelia thought, and she paused for a moment beside the pine. *I'm early, maybe two hours early, but she knows I'm coming.* A sense of wonder filled the girl.

"Come in, child," said Portia when Ophelia knocked, and she made no comment about the change in time. In the living room, instead of taking the seat Portia offered, Ophelia moved restlessly about the room. She kept her left arm still, holding the magazine, and with her right hand she touched one book and then another.

"Do you want to choose our next book?" Miss McKay asked, but Ophelia did not answer.

Finally she took a small brown volume from the shelf, *Macbeth*. "I saw this play last year at my school. A traveling company put it on. I remember Lady Macbeth washing her hands, thinking they had blood on them."

Holding the book against her chest, Ophelia dropped into a chair. "I'd like to read this. I know how Lady Macbeth felt." She looked at Portia McKay, who leaned her head on the back of her rocking chair.

"What do you mean?" the woman asked softly, and she sat up.

Ophelia took the magazine from under her arm and held it out to the woman. "Can you see the headline?"

" 'Kids Who Kill'," Portia McKay read, and she closed her eyes. "Child," she whispered, "have you done murder?"

"Yes," Ophelia answered. "There's blood on my hands, but if I ever get punished, I'll have to do it myself."

"No, oh no." Portia shook her head. Then she held her own hands in front of her. "If you have blood on your hands, you certainly have company. There's Lady Macbeth, as you mentioned. There is Pontius Pilate. And there is Portia McKay. There is blood on these hands too. I, too, have received no punishment except that which has been self-imposed. Don't punish yourself, Ophelia. The punishment of others is so much easier to bear."

Ophelia stood up. Suddenly, she did not want to be here at all. "I'll come back," she said, "but I can't stay now. I want to tell you. I just can't find the words, not today." She bent then and put the magazine in Portia's lap. "I know you can't see the print, but you can see the picture on page twenty-three. It's my brother, Roy." She smiled a little. "I loved my brother. That's why I did it."

"Yes, child," said Portia. "I understand. I loved my sister." The woman turned toward Ophelia, but the girl started to move away.

"Good-bye," she called, but the old woman moved after her.

"Wait," she called. "I want to give you something." She went to the back door and called, "Kitty, Kitty." The white ball of fur came bouncing toward her, and she swept it up. "Here." She turned back to the girl. "Mrs. Reynolds says you may have this."

Ophelia put out her hand halfway, then stopped. "I've never had a pet," she said. "My father didn't like them."

"My sister and I had a little yellow kitten," Miss McKay said softly. "But my father kicked it into the barn wall and injured it terribly. After that . . ." She paused, then changed the subject. "You take this one home with you." She handed the kitten to the girl. "You need something to love."

Ophelia stroked the soft fur. "But what if I die?" Ophelia turned away to stare out the open kitchen door. "Who will love it then?"

The question frightened Portia McKay, frightened her more than she had been frightened in three quarters of a century. Without thinking about her actions, she reached out to draw the girl to her. "Don't say such things, child," she whispered. "You won't die. You've got your whole life ahead of you."

Ophelia held the kitten between herself and the woman, but she put her other arm around Portia. "You're good to me," she said, "and you understand. No one else has ever understood." For just a second she leaned her head against Portia's tall frame, then she was out the door.

Before she left the yard, Ophelia turned back to look. The woman had risen and crossed to the window. *She's not looking out at this world*, the girl thought. *She's remembering what put the blood on her hands.* "You can't start caring too much about her, though," she said aloud. "You've got enough troubles of your own."

Ophelia moved quickly away from the woman who had stood for years at the window looking out at her guilt and away from the house that had settled long ago into the hill.

For a long time Portia McKay did not move. Evening shadows would have made it difficult even for good eyes to see out among the trees, but the woman did not care. What she saw were pictures that had flashed before her eyes for more than seventy-five years.

Four months had gone by with no sign of Daniel. Lina cried at night. "I thought he loved me," she would sob.

Portia felt sorry for her sister and almost overcome with desolation herself. There would be no getting away now. She and Lina would live always under Father's cruel hand.

"If he's not dead, he'll be back," Lina said one day, her eyes brighter than they had been before. "Maybe he just went back to Arkansas to let his wounds heal."

Portia nodded her head, but she did not believe Daniel Dunlap would ever come back. If he was lucky enough to live after that awful beating, he would be too afraid to return.

Late at night, in early November, Portia learned she had been wrong about Daniel. The tap came at the window. Portia woke first and poked her sister. "Lina, did you hear that?"

"Huh?" Lina rolled over on her back.

The tapping came again. "There! Didn't you hear that?" Portia sat up in bed.

"Yes."

The tapping came again. This time Lina sat up. She grabbed at Portia's arm. "It could be Daniel," she whispered. "Daniel might be out there." Lina threw back the quilts, ready to get out of bed.

Portia pulled her back. "Wait, you can't go to the

window! If it should be Daniel, you can't let him in here. Father would kill you and him."

"If Daniel has come back, I intend to go with him. If he'll take me, I'll go right now. I'll go in my nightgown. You will too, Porty. It's our only chance."

In the darkness Portia could not see her sister's face, but she knew how determined its expression must be.

Lina pulled away from her sister and moved toward the window. "It is Daniel," she whispered. "I knew he'd come. I knew it."

Portia heard the window open and Daniel's voice. "Come out," said Daniel. "We've got to talk."

Portia's body stiffened with fear. She pulled at the quilt to cover her head, but Lina, too, had plans for the quilt and pulled harder. The moon gave just enough light for Portia to see her sister, quilt about her shoulder, climb out the bedroom window.

Then Portia, too, was out of bed and at the window. Lina might never come back. Her sister might go off into the night wrapped in a quilt and forget to take her. Portia wanted to climb out too, but she stayed beside the window for a long time staring into the darkness. Finally she went back to bed, but not to sleep.

Just at dawn, she heard the sound of boots hitting

hard against the wooden floor. Portia sat up in bed Father! Father running through the house! Without the robe that Father always insisted be over nightgowns, she rushed barefoot into the dark hall. Father's bedroom door was open, and his massive bed was empty.

How could he have known? Father never rose until full light. Heart pounding, Portia raced to the back door. The rifle was gone from the rack, and the door ajar. She wanted to go back to her bedroom and to cover her head, but she pushed open the heavy pine door.

Her bare feet did not feel the cold as she ran over the frosty brown grass. In the pale light, she saw the open barn door. Inside Father stood with his rifle pointed at Lina and Daniel.

Portia watched as Daniel stepped in front of Lina. "Shoot me if you've got to, but don't hurt Lina. Everything was my fault." He spread his arms in an effort to shield the sobbing girl.

"Get out, daughter," Father roared. "Get yourself back to the house."

Lina moved to stand beside Daniel. "Don't shoot him, Father. Please!"

"Move away, I say."

"Go, please." Daniel gave her a little push. "I love you, Li—"

The bullet stopped his words, and Daniel crumpled to the straw-covered barn floor.

"No," screamed Lina. She whirled back to Daniel, but Father thrust the gun close to her.

"Get out!" he shouted.

Portia moved then, running to Lina and pulling her out the door. They were hardly outside when another shot sounded in the barn.

Lina put her hands to her ears and slumped against Portia. Then they saw Daniel's horse come from the barn. Lying across its back was Daniel's motionless body. Sobbing, they watched as the horse walked down the trail and disappeared among the pines.

Then father was beside them, shoving Portia away from Lina. Without a word he stomped toward the house, dragging Lina behind him.

When they were at the porch steps, Lina grabbed hold of the rail. "I won't go in the house," she said. "You can't make me. I am going to go after Daniel. You shot him."

Father jerked hard on Lina's arm, hauling her away from the rail. Then, with one quick and mighty slap, his big hand connected to her cheek. He held her arm tight, delivered another blow, and let her go. Lina reeled for a second, her golden hair flashing in the new rays of sunlight. Then she crumpled to the ground.

"Bring her in," Father ordered. He brushed by Portia without a glance backward and marched into the house. "She's likely to catch pneumonia, practically naked in this cold."

"Lina," Portia begged, "get up," but her sister did not stir. Portia dropped to the cold ground and put her arm under her sister's shoulders, pulling her up.

Lina moved her hand to her jaw. "It hurts," she whimpered. "It hurts so bad."

Portia looked back over her shoulder. "We've got to get you to the house," she said. "Father will be waiting for me to cook breakfast." Her teeth chattered from cold and from fear. "I don't know what he might do if he comes back out here. Please, Lina, please."

Lina's body felt limp to Portia, like the rag dolls they had played with as little girls, but she made her words encouraging. "That's the way. You're okay."

Getting Lina up was hard, but once up they moved more quickly than Portia had expected. She tucked Lina into their bed with a promise to come back as soon as possible.

"Dress yourself," Papa said when she rushed into the kitchen.

Surprised, Portia looked down at her gown. "Oh," she muttered. "I'll be right back."

Somehow she got through the frying of the meat and the eggs. Somehow she got Lina's face and hands washed, and a little warm tea given to her by spoon. Lina screamed when she tried to open her mouth. "I think your jaw is broken," Portia told her, "and I don't know what to do."

Father came in for the noon meal as usual. Glad that he liked the economy of leftovers, Portia heated the stew they had had for supper the night before.

"Father," she said, and she put the bowl in front of him. "I have to talk to you about Lina."

"There will be no talk of what occurred this morning." He spread his hands flat on either side of the bowl, and Portia kept her eyes on them. "Carolina must repent, of course, but there will be no talk of what happened between us."

Portia took a step back away from the table. "But her jaw is broken, I'm pretty sure. Can't we send for a doctor?"

"No, by thunder! There will be no doctor. Look among my books. You will find a volume on care of the body. It might contain a guide for care of the jaw." He pushed his chair away from the table and stood. "I have important business at the mill, but first I must tend to some things here."

He went directly from the table to the door of the girls' bedroom. *He's going in there*, Portia thought. *He might hit her again. Oh God, don't let him hit her again.*

She closed her eyes tight, opening them only when she heard the hammer. Father was nailing a bolt in place on the bedroom door. "She's to be locked in at all times until she repents," he told Portia. "You, too, at night."

Next he nailed boards over the outside of the bedroom windows. "He's going to keep you in prison," Portia whispered to her sister later. "He's going to keep us both in prison."

He didn't keep Portia locked away. "You may come and go from that room only three times during the day to take food," Seth McKay told her. "At night you will both be locked inside. I won't have my daughters cavorting with sinful men."

The next morning Portia brought breakfast to her sister, but Lina, her hand holding her face, only groaned and would not even try to eat. "Your jaw's broken," Portia said. "I read one of father's books, *Doctor Bodkin's Complete Guide to Home Treatment of the Human Body*." She took a wide strip of dark cloth from the pocket of her apron. "We've got to tie it up, but you've got to eat sometime. I'll make you some potato soup later, real thin."

"Stay with me for a while," Lina wrote on a piece of paper when Portia brought the soup, but Portia shook her head.

"He told me not to, said just bring the food and leave." She looked over her shoulder at the door. "I'm afraid of him, Lina. He might kill you."

"He killed Daniel," Lina wrote, and tears began to roll down her swollen cheek.

"I'll get a hot cloth for your face. Surely he wouldn't object if I did that."

Portia remembered the hot cloths, so hot that her hands did not lose the red scalded color between one wringing out and the next one. She kept hot cloths on her sister's face, kept the bandage tied under her chin except for the times when Lina agreed to swallow soups, broths, and milk.

Portia worried about her sister, who grew thinner and sadder with each day. "You've got to tell him you're sorry." She had stayed after bringing the thin breakfast mush to brush Lina's hair. The once-beautiful strands hung now in limp, lifeless curls.

"I'll never speak to him again. He killed Daniel, and I hate him," Lina wrote.

Portia leaned close to her sister's head. "I hate him too, but we have to live with him. Tell him you're sorry, so he'll let you out of this room. I'm afraid you might die in here."

Lina reached for the pencil. "I don't care if I die. I'm not sorry. I wouldn't be sorry for the time with Daniel. Even if that awful man does kill me, I wouldn't be sorry. I'll never call him Father again."

"But you're getting so thin and weak." Portia sobbed. "Lina, if anything happened to you, if you died, I'd be so alone."

Lina bent her head to rest it on the dresser. Her eyes were closed. There was a sound from the back of the house, a door opening. Portia put down the brush and hurried out of the room, bolting the door after her.

Portia watched her sister carefully, and worried constantly. As the weeks passed the jaw did seem to heal, but Lina did not.

She ate more now, but she often threw up what she ate. "It's the heartbreak," Portia said.

"No," said Lina, and her voice had a strange sound to it, the most despair Portia had ever heard. "No, it's more than just the sorrow."

Portia moved closer to her sister, who sat on the edge of the bed. "What? What is it, then? Why do you throw up?" She lowered herself to sit beside Lina.

"I'm not sure, but I'm afraid it's . . ." Lina began to

sob and threw herself over to lie on the bed, drawing her knees up close to her chest.

"What, Lina?" Portia stood up and leaned over her sister, pulling at her arm. "You've got to tell me what!"

Lina took her hand from across her mouth. "I haven't had my time of the month, not since November."

It took Portia a few moments to understand. Then a small scream escaped from her throat. "Lina, oh Lina, what were you and Daniel doing in that barn?" She stepped back from the bed.

Lina sat up. "Daniel and I were going to get married. I loved him, Portia. It only happened that once."

"Can a baby come after just once?" Portia moved to the window, forgetting it was boarded up and provided no view, no visual escape.

"I don't know, Portia. I don't know, but I haven't had the bleeding, not since November before I lay with Daniel."

"This is February," Portia said, "almost the end of February."

"Maybe the bleeding will come." Lina fell back onto the bed.

"It has to," Portia whispered. "Oh, Lina, it just has to."

———

That afternoon Portia saw her father kick Sunshine. She paused near a kitchen window just as her father came out of the barn to stride toward the mill. The half-grown cat ran after him.

Portia drew a sharp breath. "Don't get in his way, Sunshine," she whispered, but she saw the cat brush against her father's leg. Father paused only slightly, then turned and, with a great swing of his leg, kicked the kitten.

The yellow form flew through the air and hit the side of the red barn. Father walked on toward the mill.

For a minute Portia did not move. When she could lift her feet, she hurried out to the cat. Sunshine lay in a sad, unmoving pile. "Are you dead?" She put out her shaking hand to touch the cat.

Sunshine made a soft crying sound and lifted his head. Portia picked him up. His body felt strange in her hands. Gently, she moved her finger down his back. Sunshine meowed in pain. "Oh, kitty," Portia sobbed. "Your back must be broken."

She put the kitten on the ground. It struggled up on its front legs, but the back half of its body lay twisted on the ground. Sunshine could not move.

Crying, Portia leaned against the barn. Then, holding on to the wall, she made her way inside. The dimness after the bright light made it hard to see, but finally her eyes fell on the shovel. "There it is." She took it with her outside.

Digging the hole did not take long. Shaking, Portia picked up the cat. "I'm sorry, kitty." Should she kill it first, put it out of its misery? But how? Would Sunshine suffer more from suffocation than if she hit him with the shovel? She raised the shovel but could not hit the cat. Sobbing, she stroked its head before she lowered it into the hole.

Pitiful sounds came from the yellow cat, but Portia made herself pile the soft earth over it. Finally no sound came to her ears except the sound of her own crying.

After the shovel was back in the barn. Portia went into the house. She wanted to run in to Lina. "I killed our kitten," she wanted to say. "I had to do it."

Instead she sat, crying, at the kitchen table. Lina had been hurt enough. She'd just tell her Sunshine must have run away if Lina noticed the kitten was missing.

8.

～

Ophelia hurried away from the McKay house. The October late afternoon had a hint of coolness. Ophelia dreaded winter. She hated the cold and the barenness of the land. It had been winter on that terrible day.

Snow had fallen that day as she walked home from school. It was a Friday afternoon, and Ophelia felt good until she heard the siren. It sounded close by, breaking the silence of her snow-filled world. *Someone's hurt or real sick,* she thought, and she stood still for a moment, listenting.

Roy was already up in his room. When Ophelia opened the front door, she heard music coming from upstairs. Mama had said she planned to stop at the grocery store on her way home from work. Dinner would be late. Ophelia went out to the kitchen to make herself a peanut-butter-and-jelly sandwich.

She had just spread the grape jelly over the peanut butter when Mama burst through the back door. No grocery bags filled her arms, and the look on her face made Ophelia drop the jelly knife.

Mama barely glanced at Ophelia. "Is Roy here?" Her voice sounded strange.

"Upstairs." Ophelia moved to her mother's side. "Are you okay, Mama?"

Mama turned to look closely at Ophelia's face. "You haven't heard, have you?"

"Heard what?" Ophelia put her hand on her mother's arm.

"Two women were talking at the market. I just left my groceries there in the cart." Mama's voice broke. "It's Erick, honey. He had a wreck on the way home from school." Mom put her hands over her face.

Ophelia knew whom Mama meant, but she asked anyway. "Erick? Roy's friend Erick Waller?"

Mama nodded. "Right there by the market, at the corner. He's dead, honey. Erick turned in front of a truck, and he's dead."

"Dead?" Ophelia shook her head. Erick was Roy's friend, his only friend. He had been sixteen the week before, a few months older than Roy. He had gotten his driver's license just a few days ago. "Maybe it's a mistake. Maybe those women got mixed up."

"No. One of them saw the accident. Lots of people were talking about it. They all said Erick Waller." Mama moved away from Ophelia, moved toward the hallway.

Ophelia followed. "Don't tell Roy, Mama," she said. "Please don't."

Mama looked back for just a second. "I have to, honey. He has to know."

Ophelia watched her mother climb the stairs, knock on Roy's door, and go inside. She climbed the stairs too. Each step seemed really high.

Outside Roy's closed door, she listened. Someone turned off the music. Then she head Mama's voice, but she could not understand the words. If Roy said anything, his words were too low to hear.

When Mama came out, Ophelia got a glimpse of Roy, but he closed the door quickly. The music started again, louder than before. "He wants to be alone," Mama said. She reached out to put her arm around Ophelia and started to move toward the stairs.

Ophelia drew back. "I'll just stay up here for a while." She looked back at Roy's door. "You know, in case he wants something."

Mama squeezed her shoulder. "That's sweet, honey. I'll go down to see what I can find for dinner. There's not much in the house."

For a while Ophelia leaned against the wall outside Roy's room. Then she slid down to sit on the floor, her arms wrapped around her knees. She heard Daddy come in the back door. It wouldn't be long now till Mama called up about coming down to dinner. It didn't seem likely that Roy would want to eat. Would Daddy let Roy skip the meal? Ophelia started to chew at her fingernails.

When the dinner call came, Ophelia opened Roy's door a crack. "Dinner's ready," she said, but the music drowned out her words. She slipped inside. Roy lay on the bed, his face to the wall.

Ophelia tiptoed to the bedside, reached out, and touched her brother's shoulder. "Mama says come to dinner."

He did not turn his head to look at her. "I'm not hungry," he said. "Tell them I won't come down. There's no way they can make me."

Ophelia moved away to the door, but just before she went out, she stopped. "I'm awful sorry," she called out over the music. "I mean about Erick."

Downstairs, Daddy was already seated. Mama carried food to the table. Ophelia slipped into her place. Keeping her eyes on her plate, she said, "Roy isn't hungry. He said he won't come down."

"He will if I say he will," Daddy said, but he did not move. "Oh, well," he added with a sigh, "guess we might as well leave him up there, poor kid."

Ophelia looked up. She hadn't heard Daddy say anything kind about Roy in a long time.

Mama set two plates on the table, one of bacon and one of eggs. "I'm worried about Roy," she said. "I'm afraid Erick was his only real friend."

"Maybe he'll make other friends now," Dad said.

Mama gasped. "Joe! How can you be so cruel?" She dropped into a chair.

Daddy shook his head. "I don't mean to be cruel, Sylvia. I feel bad for the kid. I do." He shrugged. "But I can't help thinking it might be good for Roy in the long run."

"You're wrong," Mama said, but she said it softly so Daddy didn't get mad.

"I don't like having breakfast for supper," Daddy said, but he filled his plate.

Later, Mama made a peanut-butter sandwich and took it up to Roy with a glass of milk. Ophelia followed after her, and while Mama told Roy that she and Daddy were worried about him and urged him to eat, Ophelia settled unnoticed in the corner.

Mama and Roy also talked about the funeral to be held on Monday. "Is Dad going with us?" Roy asked.

Ophelia could not tell by Roy's voice if he hoped Daddy would go or if he did not want Daddy by his side.

"We haven't talked about that, honey," Mama said, "but he is concerned about you. He really loves you. You know that, don't you?"

Roy just shrugged his shoulders. "I just need to be by myself, Mama," he said.

"Okay, sweetheart. Just let us know if you need us." She bent down to kiss Roy's forehead, then left the room, but Ophelia stayed quietly in the dim corner.

Roy sat up to eat the sandwich, and his eyes fell on Ophelia. "What do you want?"

"Nothing. Just to see you, I guess." Ophelia stood up and moved closer.

"Not anything to see." He took a bite of the sandwich, but he put the rest on the plate and lay back down.

Ophelia turned to leave the room. She had her hand on the doorknob when Roy spoke.

"Hey, kid," he said. "Thanks for caring."

"I liked Erick, too," Ophelia said. "He was nice to me."

"He would have been nice to everyone if they had let him, even those idiots at school."

Ophelia nodded. "Think they'll be sorry now?"

"Yeah, they'll probably be crying all over the place, but it's too late." He rolled over and hit the pillow hard with his fist.

Later, in the middle of the night, Ophelia woke. Sleep did not come back to her. Finally, she got up and went to her window to watch the snow, which still fell in the light of the backyard security lamp.

A sound made her turn toward the door. Roy stood there silhouetted against the brightness of the hall. He held a sleeping bag under his arm. "I didn't know you were awake," he said, and Ophelia knew he was sorry that she was. "I just thought I might stay in here for a while."

"Okay," she said. She wanted to say she was glad to have him, but Roy didn't like to have a big deal made about things. She flipped on her lamp, went to the closet, and got her own sleeping bag. Before she turned off the lamp, she opened the drawer of the bedside table and took out a small object. "I'm going to plug in my night-light," she said. "I sort of like it sometimes."

"You don't have to sleep down here on the floor too," he said.

"Oh, I want to."

"They called us names," Roy said, "and just last week, they threw ketchup at us in the cafeteria, those little packages. First one hit me in the face, then Erick, right in his eye. He started rubbing his eye, and someone yelled, 'Crybaby.' I hate them." Roy's voice broke. There was enough light to see him roll over and bury his face in the pillow.

Ophelia thought probably she should leave him alone, but she couldn't without asking a question. "Why? Why are the kids so mean?"

Roy didn't answer right away, but then he rolled over. "It got to be their game, their entertainment. They called us 'homo.' They said Erick walked like a girl. They started picking on us as soon as we got to be friends." He ran his hands through his hair and went on. "Erick wasn't that way. Anyway, I don't think he was, but you know what? It didn't matter to me anyway. I was always shy. Didn't know how to joke, and I wasn't interested in sports. After about the fifth grade, all the other guys got so big. I'm so scrawny and short. For a long time, I never had a real friend. Since way back when I was little, I was just by myself at school."

"All the kids?" Ophelia asked. "Were they all mean to you."

"No," said Roy, "just the popular bunch, but you don't know what it's like after elementary school." Roy sat up, and his voice got loud. "If the important crowd doesn't like you, the others don't either. They might not throw things, but they don't look at you, either. You're just a reject."

"You're not a reject, Roy." It was all she could think to say.

When Roy spoke, his voice was quiet again, but there was a cold, hard sound to it. "Erick wasn't a reject either, but they put a note in his locker with a dollar bill. The note said, 'Start saving for your sex-change operation.' He found the note right after school. When I turned the corner in the hall, I saw them, four boys, leaning against the wall and laughing."

Roy put his hands up to cover his face. "Erick ran out. I followed him. I yelled at him to wait, but he was too far ahead to hear. I would have been with him if he had waited. Even though Dad said I couldn't ride with him, I would have been with him. He died on the way home.

"It's their fault. Maybe I'll make them pay. Just

maybe I'll show them." He took his hands away from his face and clinched them into fists.

The hardness of Roy's voice frightened Ophelia. "But they'll be sorry now. Remember? You said they'd be crying and everything."

Roy didn't say anything. He just sat there in the dark. After a while, he lay back down. Ophelia couldn't think of anything to say. She knew Roy wasn't asleep. She wanted to wait until his even breathing told her he was, but she couldn't keep her eyes open.

In the morning Roy and his sleeping bag were gone. At the top of the stairs, she paused, listening to the sounds of pans rattling in the kitchen. On Saturday mornings, if Daddy's mood was good, he liked to make pancakes for breakfast. The preparation was always loud and messy, but Mama never complained, just cleaned up after him with a smile. Daddy hadn't cooked in quite a while.

"Are you hungry?" Daddy turned from the stove and smiled at Ophelia. "I sure hope so."

"Starved," Ophelia lied. She would eat.

Mama came to the table to set out three plates just as Daddy came over with the pancakes. "Set another plate," he said. "I want Roy to come down."

Ophelia looked quickly at Mama, who frowned. "Maybe we should just let him come down when he wants to, Joe." She reached for napkins to put beside the plates.

"I want him eating with us. He's been up there by himself long enough." He slammed the pancake platter onto the table and stomped out toward the stairs.

Ophelia moved to take her place. "They'll yell at each other," she said, and her body stiffened.

Mama started putting butter on the pancakes. "I should have gone up for him before your father had a chance." She pressed her lips together tightly.

Ophelia and Mama waited, but no sounds of shouting drifted to them. Soon Daddy came back, followed by a white-faced Roy. Mama got another plate.

Daddy passed the pancakes and talked about the snowdrifts outside. "Guess you two will want to get out the sled again," he said between bites.

Ophelia looked at Roy. His lips quivered. "Dad," he said, "we don't have a sled. That one we used last year belonged to Erick."

"Oh, well, then I'd better go downtown and get you one. I can drive there. Sand trucks got out to do the streets early."

"I'm not interested in sledding today." Roy did not even look up.

"Me either," said Ophelia. With her fork, she moved the pancakes around on her plate and took little bites occasionally.

"Well, all right, then." Daddy made a sort of snorting sound after the words. "It was just an idea."

No one else at the table spoke, and Ophelia's mind filled with that day last winter, the day of the year's only big snow. The doorbell rang, and Erick stood there, his tall, thin body covered by a huge overcoat. A red stocking cap hid his green hair and his forehead. Ophelia wished Erick wore his cap always. If he covered his wild hair, maybe Daddy wouldn't complain about Roy being friends with him.

"Hey," Erick said when Roy opened the door. "It finally snowed big. I brought my sled."

All the winter before, Erick's first year in Oklahoma, he had talked about the great winter fun he'd had in Wisconsin. "Come on," he said before Roy could open his mouth. "Bring the kid, too."

Ophelia didn't wait to hear more, just hurried to get her coat and gloves. Deer Run was not a town full of hills, but they found one big enough to be fun.

The sled held one boy with just enough room left for Ophelia's smaller body. Although the boys took turns, Ophelia went on all the rides, flying down the hill with snow blowing up in her face. After the ride, she trotted back up behind one or the other of the boys. She remembered how cold her nose got, and she remembered the laughing. They had laughed, it seemed to Ophelia, all that winter afternoon.

Sitting there at the breakfast table, Ophelia wondered about the kids at Roy's school. How could they make a game of throwing stuff and calling hateful names? Erick and Roy had never hurt anyone.

Roy pushed his chair back, but Mama put out her hand and touched his arm. "Do you want to go to the funeral home, honey?"

Roy stared at her. "Why? Why would I want to do that?"

Mama stood up and put her arm around his shoulder. "I thought you might want to see Erick . . . you know, before the funeral."

"See him dead? Why would I want to see him dead?"

Dad pushed back from the table. "Wonder if the funeral home people will dye his hair back to a normal color," he said.

Roy pushed away from Mama, and his face had a wild look. He shook his fist at Daddy. "Shut your stupid mouth," he shouted. "You and that rotten bunch at school. It's mouths like yours that killed him."

He spun around toward the door, but then he whirled back, grabbed the breakfast table, and turned it over. Daddy had to jump away, and dishes flew everywhere.

"What on Earth!" Daddy yelled. Roy screamed as if someone had shot him, and he ran out of the room.

"Come back here, damn you," yelled Daddy, but Roy didn't come back.

Daddy kicked at the table and started to go after Roy, but Mama stepped in front of the door. "Joe, don't! Let him be." She spread her arms across the doorway. "If you go after him, it will have to be through me."

For a minute Ophelia thought her father would knock her mother over, but he didn't. He started pacing up and down the room. Mama motioned for Ophelia to come to the doorway, and she let her arm down just long enough for Ophelia to slip through.

For most of the day, Ophelia hung around Roy's door. He didn't come out, and when Ophelia or Mama knocked at the door, he called, "Go away." It was the same on Sunday. Mama took food in to Roy, but he kept his back turned while she was in the room.

Ophelia sat on the top stair, waiting for Mama to come out of Roy's room. "Is he okay?" she asked when Mama closed the door.

Mama sat down beside her. "He's full of so much rage." Mama shook her head. "I can't tell if he thinks Erick turned in front of that truck on purpose to kill himself or if he thinks Erick was distracted, thinking about how badly he was treated. Either way, he blames Erick's death on the kids at school. I don't see how we can force him to go back there."

Ophelia leaned against Mama. "Could we maybe move to a whole new town?" She would hate to leave her friends, but it would be worth it for Roy to get away from that awful bunch.

"I don't think your father would even consider a move. Possibly a boarding school. That might work."

"I don't want Roy to go away." Ophelia bit at her lip.

"We have to think of what's best for him, darling." Mama got up and went down the stairs.

Roy came out on Monday morning dressed in church clothes—dark pants and a maroon sweater. Ophelia thought he looked awful nice, but she knew he didn't want to hear that. She was glad Daddy had already left for work so there was no worry about the shouting starting.

"I knew he wouldn't go," Roy said. "Who needs him anyway?"

Ophelia had never been to a funeral. When they got out of the car at the church, she hung back to be behind Mama and Roy. A group of girls stood nervously around the sidewalk. "Kristy should be here by now," one of them said. Ophelia noticed that some of the girls wiped at their red eyes with tissue. Maybe Roy would be comforted by how many kids seemed to be sorry about Erick's death.

Two boys walked up to the girls, and Ophelia stopped walking to listen to the conversation. She heard one of the boys say, "What's all the blubbering for?" He grinned. "We're just here because we're out of school for the morning, so our folks griped at us to come. None of us could stand the weirdo."

Mama had walked on, but Ophelia realized that Roy had stepped back to take her arm. "You're not even a human being, are you, Hodges?" Roy said.

Josh Hodges poked the boy beside him. "Hey, the

homo's carrying on about something, like anyone would ever listen to anything he says." With a little laugh he turned around to move toward the church steps.

"Don't pay any attention to them," Ophelia whispered. As she and Roy walked on, Ophelia felt him shaking beside her.

Mama waited for them at the church door, and they walked in together. A man who seemed to be directing people spoke softly to Roy. "A place has been reserved for classmates at the front," he said.

"I don't want to sit with them," Roy said, and he followed Mama to a pew. All through the service, he sat with arms folded, back and neck straight.

When the funeral was over, he turned to Mama and Ophelia. "Let's go home," he said.

"Don't you want to go to the cemetery, honey?" Mama asked.

Roy's hands were made into fists again, and he poked them into the pockets of his dress pants. "No, I can't take it anymore. They're burying Erick on that hill." He closed his eyes. "I heard someone say so. You can see the high school from that hill. I hate that. I really hate that."

Both the high school and cemetery were at the edge of town, not far from Ophelia's house. Only a fence with vines separated the school grounds from the cemetery. The kids made jokes about how some of the teachers were really dead and had been dropped off on the wrong side of the fence.

"Are you sure you don't want to go to the burial?" Mama put her hand on Roy's arm. "You might be sorry later."

Roy shook his head. "I won't be sorry, but some other people might." He turned and hurried out of the church. Mama and Ophelia followed.

On the way home he sat in the backseat with his arms still folded tightly in front of him. Ophelia thought he looked as if he were holding something tightly inside.

"Are you sure you'll be okay here alone?" Mama said when she was ready to go back to work. "I can stay if you need me."

Ophelia shook her head. Music came from upstairs. "Roy'll probably just stay in his room the rest of the day."

"If you want to go to school, sweetheart, I'll stay home."

"No," said Ophelia. "I don't feel like going to school."

"If you need anything, just run over to Grandma's."

"We'll be okay, Mama."

Mama kissed Ophelia on the cheek, looked one last time up the stairs toward Roy's room, then went out the door. Ophelia drifted back up to her room, but she had barely reached the top when Roy came bursting out his door.

"Mama's gone, huh?" His voice was full of excitement, and his eyes flashed.

"Yes, she just left."

"Good!" He dashed down the steps.

Ophelia ran after him. "What's up? Where you going?"

Roy did not answer, just rushed through the living room and into the den. He stopped in front of a glass case.

Ophelia knew even before he put out his hand. She knew with a terrible certainty. "Don't," she screamed. "Please don't mess with Daddy's guns."

"I've had it. I decided when I heard what Josh Hodges said," he said. "I'm through with taking it."

Roy put out his hand and tried the door. Of course, Ophelia thought, Daddy always kept the cabinet locked and he had the key on his key ring. But Roy whirled around, moved to the bookcase, and snatched up a heavy glass bookend made in the shape of a globe.

Ophelia put her hands over her face, but she heard

the crash. When she took away her hands, Roy was reaching into the cabinet to undo the latch.

"What are you going to do?"

He swung a rifle over one shoulder and tucked a pistol into his pants waist. "I'm going to take these guns to the cemetery, where Erick is. I'll wait behind the fence, and I'm going to show them they can't push us around anymore. I don't want them up there, ever, bothering him. When they change classes and go up to the gym, I'm going to show them."

Ophelia stepped toward her brother. "Please, Roy," she begged. "Put those guns back. You don't want to hurt anyone. Please."

"I'm not going to hurt anyone. Don't worry. I'll shoot over their heads. I know what I'm doing, I just want to show them they can't push us around anymore. That's all."

"I'll call Daddy." Ophelia turned and started for the phone.

"Wait." Roy followed her and grabbed her arm. "Don't try to stop me." He let go of her arm, pulled out the pistol, and aimed the gun at his head. "If you do, if anyone tries to stop me, I'll just shoot myself."

Ophelia did not take another step toward the phone. "You shouldn't do this," she begged, but Roy hurried out of the room, through the kitchen, and toward the door.

"No." He stopped, and Ophelia thought for an instant that he had changed his mind, but he only whirled back toward the front hall. "I'll get my coat. It's cold. Besides, I'll need my coat to put over the guns."

Ophelia followed him as far as the stairs and then sank onto the bottom step.

Roy had his long coat then, and he stuck the rifle under it. "Don't tell," he said to Ophelia just before he went out the front door. "You do, and I'll blow my head off."

When he was gone, she leaned against the door. Her heart raced and sweat ran down from her forehead. What should she do? If she called Daddy and he showed up at the school or even called the school, Roy might really kill himself. Ophelia bit at her lip until she tasted blood.

She tried to move away from the door, but her legs were shaky and she made it only to the stairs, where she dropped into a trembling heap.

9.

Portia McKay made her way down the road. She could no longer sit in the house, waiting. Two weeks had passed with no visit from Ophelia.

"Don't know what's troubling that girl," Bernice Reynolds had said when she came about the groceries. "Just stays in her room all the time." The woman sighed. "Oh, these fosters! You never can tell."

Portia didn't know why she had finally left her post by the window and come out to walk the road. "Are you going to pound on her door?" she asked herself, and she bent to pick up a stone to roll about in her hand.

"Wouldn't do any good, my going over there." She squeezed the stone hard in her hand. "People have come to my door aplenty. Never did any of them any good, did it?" She tossed the stone away.

"Go on home," she told herself. "Go home and hope. It's all you can do except maybe pray." She had not prayed in so many years, not since the night the baby came.

The November afternoon sun felt warm on her body, but the day she remembered, that terrible July day, had been unbearably hot.

Portia noticed that she relied more on her cane as she moved toward home. Were her steps becoming more shaky? Her father had been a strong walker until he was almost one hundred. From her father, Portia had inherited genes for long life.

She wondered about her mother. How long might Mama have lived had she not died from complications after a miscarriage? How different might Portia's own life have been had her mother and the baby boy she had carried lived?

Childbirth was a killer in Portia's family. It had claimed the lives of her mother and her sister, and of course her own. There was no doubt that childbirth had claimed Portia's life too.

Suddenly in late February, Father had announced that Lina had likely learned her lesson and unlocked the bedroom door. "Too much work to be done around here in the springtime—he had to let me go," Lina commented.

By the end of March, when most of the trees were leafing out, Lina knew for certain what she had feared was true. Her body could not deny the child that grew within it, and she told her sister on a spring day as they hung wash on the line.

"It's true," she said. "And when he discovers the fact, he will kill me."

"He won't discover it," said Portia through clenched teeth. "We have to make sure he doesn't."

Lina put her hand on her stomach. "We can't hide a baby." She shook her golden curls. "He will have to know. Someday soon, he will know."

"No, he won't." Portia spread a pair of her father's overalls on the line. "We'll think of something. We have to."

Lina's face grew thinner, more strained, as her middle grew larger. As they always did in spring, the girls made two new dresses for each of them, both with shirts that fell full from fitted bodices.

Dresses were one part of their lives that Father had never cared to direct. Early on he had left clothing to a neighbor woman hired to sew for them and later to teach them to make their own garments.

"He'll never notice your stomach," Portia said. "Not if we both wear full dresses."

Portia believed she was right; she did not believe Father noticed. Lina feared otherwise. "I think he knows," she whispered one night after they had gone to bed. "I think he knows. Sometimes I catch him looking at me with a strange expression. I think he knows, and he is waiting to see what we do. He knows, and he is watching us, like a cat with a mouse." A shudder went through her body that even Portia, beside her, could feel.

"We'll think of something," Portia said. "I know we will."

Long after Lina had gone to sleep, Portia lay staring into the night. If Papa knew or if he found out, he would beat Lina until she died. Of that fact Portia had no doubt. She could imagine him thundering into their room, grabbing Lina's arm with his massive hand, and jerking her from the bed. He would have his great whip in his other hand, and he would use the whip to kill Lina instead of shooting her as he had Daniel Dunlap. In her mind Portia could see her sister's lifeless body as Papa threw it against the wall.

After Lina's dead, she thought, *he won't touch her again. It will be up to me to move her, to somehow get her out of the house and to dig a grave for her.* It would be that way, Portia knew, unless she thought of a way to save her sister.

As spring came on, Portia could see that her sister's breasts grew heavy, but she did not think that was a fact likely to be noticed by her father.

Portia McKay's mind came back to the present. She had reached the spot on the road where the path led to the river. No, she would not make her way down the hill to the edge of the water. The incline had been hard for her to maneuver the last time she had gone there, and she did not have the energy today. She peered toward the path. That last trip had been just before the girl, Ophelia, had come to read for the first time. Portia had not seen the rock, had not sat on it, since the new golden girl had come into her life.

Could the girl be there on the rock now? No. She shook her head. If the girl were on the rock, Portia believed she would sense her presence. Rain had fallen again last night, and the water's roar hurt Portia's ears. She hoped Ophelia would stay away from that river.

10.

Ophelia shivered and zipped her blue coat. Where was the school bus? Mrs. Reynolds had said the weatherman predicted an ice storm today, but nothing fell yet. For more than two weeks she had stayed away from Miss McKay's. She had become too close to the old woman. Ophelia knew she couldn't let herself really care about anyone again. She was not meant to ever care for anyone again. She supposed that was part of her punishment. She would find Miss McKay dead if she let herself care.

She had all she needed from the old woman anyway, enough money for a one-way trip home. No need for a ticket back. Some social worker would come and find her, but first she would surely have time to stand on the sidewalk in front of the house once more and go to the cemetery.

A yellow bus slowed to a stop, and Ophelia climbed on. Before English class she stood at her locker, half dreading, half looking forward to seeing Mark Haines. Just the day before, he had come right over to her before class. "You must know by now that I like you, Ophelia. Will you go out with me?"

Ophelia had felt her face begin to burn. "I live in a foster home," she said softly, and kept her eyes down.

"So? They have to let you out sometimes, don't they? Come on, say you'll go out with me."

Ophelia thought later that if she hadn't looked up, had not seen that goofy smile that reminded her somehow of a St. Bernard puppy, she might not have said such a foolish thing. But she did look up, and she did see the smile.

"Maybe I'll ask," she said so low that Mark had to lean close to hear.

"Good deal," Mark practically shouted just as the teacher came in. Ophelia decided the best thing to do today was to walk to class slowly and go in with Miss Talley. Still, she couldn't keep from returning Mark's smile as she slipped into her seat.

Ophelia took a deep breath and relaxed, but as soon as Miss Talley began to speak, all relaxation was gone. "We are going to the library today to work on the research paper that was assigned last week," the teacher announced. "How many of you have decided on a topic for your papers? They don't have to be long, but I want you to use at least two magazine articles as sources for your information. You can use the *Readers' Guide* to look up ideas."

Ophelia squirmed in her seat. What if she hadn't stolen the magazine? Someone in the class would have been sure to see the article.

She pulled her mind to what was happening. One of the girls talked of writing about horses. Ophelia had no ideas. Nothing interested her. Then Mark Haines put up his hand.

"I want to do mine on violent kids," he said, and Ophelia's body began to shake. "I saw an article last spring about a kid right here in Oklahoma who killed people a few years ago. I went into the library yesterday, but Mrs. Burris and I couldn't find the magazine. She said she knew where she could get one, though, and she'll have it for me this morning. Hey, do I get extra points for being renacious?"

Some of the kids laughed, but Miss Talley frowned at them. "The word is tenacious, Mark, but I believe you know that. No, you do not get points for your weak attempt to entertain."

Some of the kids laughed again. This time Miss Talley did not frown at them. Ophelia fought the vomit that threatened to rise from her stomach.

She glanced quickly at the door. What if she just walked off? If she ran away they would come for her. Would they find her even if she made it into the hills that surrounded the town?

Of course, she would die eventually from starvation. How long did it take for a person to die of starvation? It didn't take as long to die from exposure, but the November nights were not yet cold enough for that. Maybe by December.

Ophelia shook her head. They would find her by December. They would surely have dogs and hundreds of people tramping around looking for her, and helicopters flying low. Undoubtedly it would be Mark Haines who found her.

She could imagine herself hiding among some dried-out underbrush. Mark would uncover her and pull her out. "Hey," he would say, "no need to get so bent out of shape. I just want you to answer some questions for the class after I do my report. You know, things like, why'd your brother kill people?"

Mark would be smiling at her the whole time. Mark would not want to harm her, Ophelia was sure of that. He wasn't hateful like the kids who had tormented Roy and Erick, but still Mark Haines made her desperate—desperate enough to do almost anything.

"I'm sick," she said, and she ran from the room with her hand over her mouth. It was not a lie. There was no school nurse here. She'd go to the office and say she had thrown up in the rest room. Later she'd figure out what to do next. At least she would not be in the library when Mark Haines opened that magazine.

No one answered the phone at the Reynolds house. For an hour, Ophelia lay on a cot in a small room off the office. She kept her body still and her eyes closed, but her heart and mind raced. She had just about decided to try sneaking out when the school counselor came in. "I think you can go back to class now, Ophelia," she said.

Ophelia did not argue. Without a word, she got up from the cot, walked to her locker, took her history book, and headed to class.

Mark was there already in his seat, and he glanced

up at her as she entered the room. She did not look directly at him, but as soon as she sat down he turned around. "I saw your brother's picture," he said, "in a magazine about kid murderers." He smiled a little at her. "I'm not doing the report," he said.

Ophelia did look at him then, searching his face. Was he saying he would keep her secret? "Do you mean you won't tell anyone?" Waiting, she held her breath.

"Well . . ." He hesitated. "That's the thing. When I opened the magazine, we were in the library. It was a surprise, you know, seeing your name and all." He stopped and looked down at his hand on the back of the desk. "I got up and went off by myself. I was real interested, and I didn't know a couple of the guys had come to look for me. They looked over my shoulder and read part of the story."

"Oh." She opened her history book and got out her paper.

"Listen." Mark reached out to close her book. "Don't let this get you down. You didn't do anything wrong. You don't have to be ashamed."

Ophelia opened her book again. "It doesn't matter. I won't be here after today."

Mark's voice was full of concern. "Are they moving you?"

"No."

"What, then?"

Ophelia picked up her book and slammed it hard against the desk. "Look it up in *Hamlet*. You seem to be really good at looking stuff up."

"I'm sorry, Ophelia. I like you a lot. I'm awful sorry." He ran his hand through his hair.

Ophelia sighed. "I am sorry too," she said. "I shouldn't have yelled at you. You've been nice to me. I don't want you to feel bad after I go away."

"Mark Haines," said the history teacher, "will you please turn around."

Ophelia had not realized that the bell had rung. She moved her head to look around at the other kids. *They're wondering about me*, she thought. No one said anything until lunch. In the cafeteria, there were no empty tables. Ophelia sat down beside Jamie, a quiet girl she recognized from geometry class.

"Hi," Jamie said. She smiled, but she did not look at Ophelia. She jabbed quickly at her macaroni and cheese with her fork.

With a sigh, Ophelia set down the milk carton she had opened. "I guess you've heard about me." Her voice sounded tired, and she leaned against the cafeteria table.

"Gosh." Jamie's face twisted. "It must be awful

hard for you." She looked up then, but it was too late. Ophelia stood up, walked away from the table, and left her tray.

Not many kids stood around in the hall, just four or five outside the cafeteria door. The group laughed and talked, but they grew quiet as Ophelia came near them. Her heart raced, and her feet wanted to do the same. *Don't run,* she told herself. *You've got to stay here until school is out. If you run away now, they will just come after you. Wherever you run, they will come after you.*

She headed down the hall toward her locker. When it was open, she surveyed the contents. Was there anything in there she wanted to take with her, anything she didn't want the school authorities to find after she was gone?

An orange book on the top shelf caught her eye. *Hamlet.* She did not want to leave the book. She did not want old Miss McKay's book left here at school. Hadn't she promised to return the book? She reached for the orange volume.

Three afternoon classes had yet to be faced. In each one she slipped into her seat and sat hunched miserably, waiting for class to begin.

Ophelia did not listen to any of the lessons. In science the teacher mentioned a test and kids hurried to take notes on topics that the teacher mentioned, but Ophelia did not care.

"Ophelia," said Mr. Cline, "why aren't you taking notes?"

She shrugged her shoulders and picked up her pencil. "I will," she said, "but I won't be back to this school after today."

Mr. Cline went on giving notes. On her paper Ophelia wrote "I am getting out of here." She wrote the sentence over and over.

In geometry she pretended to work, but made lines on her paper without thinking. Her mind filled with the orange book she had taken from her locker. She would ride home on the bus and tell Mrs. Reynolds that she was going to see Miss McKay. It was a good plan, one that would keep Mrs. Reynolds from calling someone to say Ophelia was missing.

Before she left Miss McKay, she would tell the old woman exactly what had happened to her five years ago. Sitting in geometry class, Ophelia decided she would tell her story aloud just once before she did what she had to do.

11.

~~~~~~~

By the time Ophelia got off the bus that afternoon, a thin mist of ice had begun to fall. Ophelia feared Mrs. Reynolds might protest her trip to Miss McKay's, but she felt relieved to find her foster mother on the phone. Mrs. Reynolds waved Ophelia on, and she was soon out the door.

"I've come to return your book," she said when Miss McKay opened the door for her.

The old woman peered at the girl closely. "You didn't come to read, then?" She still held open the screen door, and Ophelia walked inside even though she had already handed *Hamlet* to the woman.

"I shouldn't even come in, because I'm in a hurry," she said, but she did not turn back.

"In a hurry to do what?" Miss McKay walked

through the kitchen and headed toward the living room. Ophelia followed.

"I'm leaving," she said, "but I guess I want to tell you something first."

"Sit down, child, and tell me what you're talking about." Miss McKay took her usual rocking chair, and Ophelia settled on the end of the couch. She did not take off her coat. "Now, where is it that you are going? Are they moving you to a different home?"

"Not exactly." Ophelia did not meet the woman's eyes. "I'm just leaving, that's all, but I want to tell you."

"It is good, I think, to tell the tale." Portia leaned back in the chair and closed her eyes, and Ophelia was glad not to have those burning pieces of coal watching her.

Ophelia took a deep breath and began in a strong voice. "My brother took some guns to school, and hid behind a fence with vines in it. He shot a bunch of times, but he didn't really mean to hit anyone." Her voice grew softer. "He did, though. He killed a boy."

She stood up and began to walk about the room. "I knew he had the guns. I could have told someone, but that's not the worst thing I did."

The old woman sat up and leaned forward in her

chair. "What is it, Ophelia? Tell me why you think you have blood on your hands."

"Roy, that was my brother's name . . . Anyway, he ran home. He got there just a few minutes before the police. 'They'll come for me,' he said."

Ophelia stopped walking and looked at Miss McKay. "Do you understand? I loved my brother. I loved him so much."

"Oh, yes, child. I understand so well." Tears she had not felt in years rolled down the old woman's cheeks.

"We heard them at the door, pounding. Roy started to get in the broom closet, but I said, 'No, they'll look there." Then I opened the cabinet under the kitchen sink. Roy got in there. He had to squeeze up a whole bunch, but he got in there, and he took the pistol in there too. See, Roy was little. He was real little for fifteen, not much bigger than me, and I was only ten." Ophelia stopped as if the story were over.

"Go on," said Portia. "Go on and tell me."

"The police looked everywhere. There were three of them. They made me stay in the hall while they looked. When they went in the kitchen, I wanted to scream, but I didn't. I just stood there, and I prayed they wouldn't find Roy. I thought about if it was right or not to pray that he wouldn't be found, but I did pray anyway. Like I said, I loved Roy a lot, more than anyone else in the world except my mama." She moved back to the couch and sat down.

I heard them open the broom closet, but they never did look under the cabinet. I guess they just thought it was too small a place, or maybe they thought there were shelves there. I don't know, but they didn't look. Mama and Daddy came home while the police were looking.

Daddy was so mad. He was even mad at me like he knew it was my fault, but he didn't know. If he had known, he would have told the police. The policemen went outside and left us alone. One stayed by our front door, and one stayed by the back door, but they didn't come back inside until later, after it was all over.

"I should have told them where Roy was, but I didn't. Daddy was ranting and raving in the living room, and Mama was there too. I went in to whisper to Roy not to come out."

Portia saw Ophelia begin to shake. The old woman wanted to get up, wanted to go to sit beside the girl, but she didn't. She was afraid Ophelia might stop talking and run.

"I didn't know Mama had come in too. She saw me bend down by that cabinet, saw me whisper." Ophelia put her hand across her eyes as if she could block the image in her mind. " 'Come out of there, Roy,' Mama said. Then everything happened so quick. Daddy was there, and he jerked opened the door. Roy didn't come out. He pointed the gun out right at Daddy.

"Daddy walked toward the gun. 'Stay away or I'll shoot you,' Roy said. I remember those words: 'I'll shoot you.'

"Daddy didn't stay back. 'Come out of there, you little fool,' he yelled, and he reached down toward Roy.

"Mama said something about how Daddy should wait, and she sort of pushed him aside. But it was too late. Roy had already pulled the trigger, and Mama fell.

"Roy went wild then. 'I killed her! I killed my own mother,' he screamed! Then he started shooting again, and Daddy fell too.

"The policemen were there by then with their guns on Roy and yelling that he should throw out his gun and then come out himself. He didn't, though. He didn't drop the gun. He just turned it to his head and shot. Then Roy fell partway out from under the cabinet.

"So there I was with just the policemen. Everyone in my family was dead on the floor, and I just stood there. I didn't even say it was all my fault. I didn't tell them that I could have stopped it."

"It wasn't your fault," said Portia. "You were just a frightened child. Believe me, I know what frightened children do. Listen to me. You shouldn't let what you did as a frightened child ruin your life."

Ophelia stood up then. "I don't have a life to ruin. I might as well have died back there with my family. I wish I had." She began to move toward the door, and the woman followed. "Now they know at this school too. The social workers won't move me, but that's okay. I am too tired to move anyway. I'm tired of having people talk about what happened, and I'm just tired of everything."

It was then that Miss McKay reached out to touch Ophelia just as she had on the last visit. She put her hand on the girl's arm. "Where are you going, child? Don't run away. They'll just bring you back."

Ophelia opened the door and stepped out. "They can't bring me back, not from where I'm going."

She was gone then, a blond girl in a blue coat, hurrying over the path that led into the trees. For a long time Portia McKay stayed shivering on the screen porch. She looked down at her hand, remembering how she had reached out to touch the girl. How strange it was to willingly touch another human being. She had touched the old man, her father. When he was very old and very sick, she had been forced to wash him, to help him move from place to place. It had been a revolting thing to touch him. It had been, she told herself, part of her punishment, part of the years and years of punishment.

Portia could no longer see the blue coat, but she did not go inside. The girl's words had frightened her. What had she meant about how she couldn't be brought back from where she was going? There could be only one place from which Ophelia could not be brought back.

"She's planning to kill herself." The words came from Portia's mouth in an anguished whisper, and she turned her head in the direction of the river. "Don't just stand here. You can't let another golden girl die. You've got to stop her."

Portia whirled and went back into her house. For the first time ever, she wished for a telephone. She took her heavy brown coat from the peg near the kitchen door, grabbed her cane, and headed back out the door.

The cold wind did not worry Portia, but the icy mist it carried did. Already the doorstep had slick spots. She stood, holding on to the screen door, and thought. Should she go on? The walk to the river was mostly downhill, not easy even without the ice. If she should be injured in a fall, she would, in all likelihood, lie there until she froze to death.

Her eyes looked out into the darkening afternoon. " 'It seems to me most strange that men should fear death, a necessary end that will come when it will come.' You see, Father, I remember my Shakespeare." Another child would not die at that river, not if she could help it. She inched down from the icy steps, then moved more quickly across the grass.

How many times had she made this trip down to the river? With each rocky step she remembered. During the sweltering summers of her childhood, she had run down this road. The river had been a delight then, cool and fresh against her burning skin.

During her fourteenth summer, she and the river had both changed. On that night, on the date carved into rock, the river had become her dreadful partner, and its waters were never again a pleasure to her.

Lina's pains had started early in the morning, before dawn. Portia woke to Lina's hand on her shoulder. "I'm hurting," she said.

Portia sat up at once. "How bad?"

"Not too bad, but it definitely hurts. It's going to come, Portia. This baby's going to be born."

"It's too soon. I thought we'd have more time." Portia jumped from the bed.

"What are we going to do?" Lina sat up.

"We'll have to run away. I've been thinking about it. We'll steal the wagon and run away."

Lina shook her head. "He'd catch us. You know he would. He'd close the mill and have every man out after us."

Portia paced across the room. "Maybe he will catch us, but we've got to try. It's our only chance."

"He'll catch us, and he'll kill us." Lina lay back down, and she began to sob.

Portia ignored the comment for which she had no answer. Maybe an idea would come to her yet. "We can hide the birthing." She moved over to light the bedside lamp. "You leave that part to me. As for keeping the secret from Father, I guess we'll just have to pray."

Portia took the big medical book from beneath the bed and settled with it near the lamp to read again what was written about the pains. Lina dozed off while Portia read. When she had finished, Portia closed the book and sat watching her sister sleep. While she watched, she planned.

"Lina's sick," she told Father at breakfast. "She's throwing up something awful."

Father frowned, but he said nothing. Portia turned away from him, back to the stove, and she smiled. There was no danger Father would go in to see Lina. Father did not care for sick people, especially sick people who had the bad manners to do something like vomit.

All day Portia went about her work of canning tomatoes from the garden, but she went in often to check on Lina. The pain was worse now. Portia washed Lina's red face and smoothed back her hair that was wet with sweat. "We've got to get you out of here," Portia said. "Father will be coming in for his supper. I've got cold meat and bread laid out."

Portia left her sister's bedside and began to pace back and forth across the room. "The thing is, you might scream, and of course the baby's bound to cry. You can't stay here in this room."

Lina whimpered, but she said nothing. Portia knew it was her problem alone. Lina hurt too much to help with the planning.

Portia moved to the window and stared out at the trees. "Lina," she said slowly, "do you think you can walk?" Lina did not answer, and Portia went to her sister, stroked her face, and asked again, "Can you walk?"

"I . . . I don't know. I think so."

Portia squeezed Lina's shoulder. "There's a wheelbarrow out back. I could push you some of the way. I'll tell Father that I want to take you down to the water. He'll most likely want to come in here to look at you. You know, to make sure we aren't trying to sneak around for some reason."

Portia took a deep breath. "Don't let him see your stomach sticking out. And don't worry—you sure look feverish."

Her father's steps at the back door made her hurry into the kitchen.

"I've got a cold supper for you, Papa, because it's so hot. There's chocolate cake, too. I've laid it all out in the dining room," she said.

Seth McKay only grunted and crossed the room to the stand, where he began to wash his hands.

"I'm worried about Lina," Portia continued, and the concern in her voice was real. "She's really feverish. Do you think maybe we ought to go for the doctor?"

"Not yet. There's not much he could do for summer complaint anyway. If she's still got the fever tomorrow, I might send one of the hands down to town to get the doctor."

"Well," Portia paused as if to think, her forehead

wrinkled while she recited her planned speech. "It's true Doc Walters didn't do much for me last summer when I had that diarrhea and vomiting."

Seth McKay's face twisted with distaste. "I'm about to have my evening meal, daughter."

"I'm sorry, Father. I think I'll take Lina down to the water. I'll fix her a place where I can cool her skin."

"I'll close the kitchen door, then, if you plan to bring her through here." He headed toward the dining room. "I don't relish seeing a sick girl limping across the room while I eat."

When the door was closed, Portia rushed back into the hall to Lina, who was curled up with pain. "You've got to get up," Portia urged. "We've got to get you out of here quick. That baby could come any minute." She wore an apron, and she patted the large pockets. "I've got what we need in here." She looked at the medical book, then shoved it back under the bed. There should be a good moon tonight, like the one the evening before, but there would not be enough light for reading. *Oh God*, Portia prayed in her mind. *Let me remember what it says*, but as she prayed she helped Lina from the bed. There was no time to stop, not even for praying.

Lina could hardly stand, and getting through the

kitchen and down the back steps was not easy. Lina kept her hand over her mouth to force back groans, and she leaned heavily on her sister.

Portia had pushed the wheelbarrow near the house. She spread a quilt across the rough bottom and helped Lina to lie back into it with her legs hanging over the front. "I don't think you can move me. I'm so heavy now." Lina could barely get out the words.

"I can do it," Portia said, and amazingly she could.

The old woman leaned against a sycamore tree, remembering the great struggle. Her pulse raced when she remembered. Even after more than seventy years that terrible night still held the power to make her shake. She wiped the dampness of melted ice from her face and moved on. This night presented its own horror. She could not block her memories, but neither could she let them slow her. She moved on, slowly, down in the direction of the water.

They had made it somehow into the trees. "We can stop now," she said when Lina cried out in pain.

For a time Portia thought she would have to somehow dump her sister from the wheelbarrow, but finally she was able to pull Lina out and keep her on her feet long enough to spread the quilt on the ground.

"We're ready for a baby." Portia knelt beside Lina and hoped that her sister did not notice how shakily the words came out.

The pains came now, one on top of the other. Lina screamed and bit her lip; the blood ran down her chin to mix there with the sweat and tears. Portia, holding her sister's hand, cried too. "It will be all right," she murmured between sobs, but she doubted her own promise.

As Portia had predicted, the moon was big and round in the sky. It cast its glow through the trees and lighted the strange scene below them. Even when she was an old, old woman, Portia would never forget the brightness of that moon and never, never observe a full moon without a pain closing tightly about her heart.

There was no moonlight now as the old woman made her way to the river. It was a journey she had taken often, and Portia McKay moved from memory more than from sight. Using her cane in front of her as a blind person does to check the ground before her, she made slow time in the trees where the ground was sheltered some from the falling mist of ice. Then she came to the road, and her movements slowed even more.

"You've got to get there before it's too late," she said aloud, but she could move no faster. "What will you do?" she asked herself. "Even if it isn't too late, even if Ophelia has not thrown herself into that icy water, how will you stop her?" Portia shook her head to show she had no answer to her own question. But she pushed herself on, willing herself not to fall.

Portia remembered Ophelia's words: "I want to tell you." *Maybe*, Portia thought, *I should tell that child my secret, so like hers, but far darker. If I find her still alive, could it make any difference if I told her my story?*

A small, icy rock beneath Portia's foot moved, and she fought for her balance, dropping her cane and waving her arms wildly. She struggled, and she won, staying upright. She retrieved her cane and moved on without resting. It was not a long trip through the trees and then over a few feet on the icy road, not a long trip. To Portia, however, it always seemed long, always since that long-ago summer night.

———

It's coming," Lina had screamed, and Portia had forced herself to look.

"Oh, God," she screamed. "I see the head."

Lina screamed again, but after the scream, she spoke. There was a sudden calmness in her words. "Catch my baby, Portia," she said. "Catch my baby, and be gentle with it."

Then the baby was there, there in the moonlight, a little girl baby in the moonlight. "Oh, Lina," Portia whispered, "she's beautiful, so beautiful."

The baby cried right at once. "She's fine," Portia said. "She's just fine. In a minute, I'll be able to cut the cord."

Portia remembered how she had worried about the scissors carried in her apron pocket. She had boiled them as the book said, but she knew they were not sterile now. She remembered thinking how she should have boiled the cloth in which she had wrapped the scissors, but she had not thought of it in time. She had so much to think of.

Lina held up her arms. "Let me hold her," she said. "Please let me hold her now."

Portia laid the baby, still crying, across Lina's breast.

"Don't cry, little girl," Lina crooned. "Oh, Portia, what are we going to do?"

Portia knelt beside her sister. "We've got to try to run away. It probably won't work, but it's the only chance we have."

"I'm too tired to move," Lina said. "You take the baby now and clean her up." She closed her eyes.

Portia took the slippery baby from her sister's arms. "You rest now, Lina. I'll take her down to the water and wash her. Maybe I'll get a good idea while I'm down there."

Portia moved through the trees. In her mind she heard her sister crying as she moved ever so slowly down that icy hill toward the river.

"It won't happen again," she said aloud. "Oh, God, don't let it happen again."

The prayer came out without having been planned, and Portia's own words startled her. She had not prayed in a very long time. Since that night, the night of July 19, 1921, Portia McKay had felt unworthy of prayer.

She found herself then at the bottom of the slope, and the trees parted. She rested just a second, breathing deeply and leaning on her cane. The rock, Portia knew, was in front of her. The darkness obscured her view of the rock beside the water, but suddenly from somewhere came enough light for her to see the outline of the girl.

Portia's hand flew to her mouth. Ophelia stood on the rock, and the sound of the raging water at her feet filled the night.

The girl looked out over the water. *She doesn't know I'm here*, Portia thought. *What do I do now?* She inched her way closer to the rock. The grass was not so hard to walk on, and with the help of her cane, the woman came near the girl before she spoke.

"Ophelia," she said. "I've come to tell you something."

"What! What did you say?" The girl turned suddenly, and for one black moment Portia McKay held her breath, sure Ophelia would lose her balance.

The woman wanted to call to the girl to be careful, but instead she watched, silent, as Ophelia's form swayed for an instant, then stilled.

Don't try to talk her out of this, Portia thought, *not at first.* "You told me your story," she said. "It seems only fair that you hear mine. I want to tell you about my sister and her baby."

"You said I look like your sister did."

She remembers. Portia felt encouraged. "You do," she said. "My sister was seventeen when I saw her last, and she was a golden girl, like you, all blond sunshine. Her baby would have grown up to look like that too. I could see that in the light of the moon on the night she was born."

"The night your sister died, right? You said she died in childbirth."

She's interested, Portia thought. *Oh, God, let me interest her enough to get her off that rock.* "Lina died after she gave birth to her second child, but that was later. She had run away by that time. Without my father's permission, she had gone off to get married, and Father would never allow her back into the house.

"Daniel, the boy Lina ran away with, had been shot by my father months before when Father caught him with Lina—shot and almost killed. It took Daniel nearly a year to recuperate and likely a while to get up his courage, but he came back for Lina. He hid in the woods and waited until he saw Father drive away to town.

"He appeared at our door with the same felt hat in his hand and the same smile in his brown eyes, but he had a new limp in his leg from one of Father's bullets. The other bullet had hit his chest, but miraculously, there he was on our porch alive.

"I saw him first, and I screamed. Then Lina was there in his arms, crying and kissing him.

" 'Grab a few things, ladies,' he said. 'We're going to shake the dust of this sawmill off our shoes!'

"Lina ran into the bedroom to get her things, but I just stood there. 'Come on, Porty,' she called. 'Get your new dress.'

"I followed her into the bedroom. 'I'm not going,' I said.

"She dropped the nightgown she had in her hands. 'Oh, yes, you are,' she said. 'Of course you are. Daniel wants you to live with us. I can't leave you here.'

" 'I'm not going.' I could hardly get the words out.

"Daniel came in to talk to me. 'There's nothing for you here except that horrible old man. We want you with us.'

"I couldn't talk, just shook my head, no. You see, Lina never knew that I had already decided to stay always with that horrible old man, our father. I promised myself to stay at his side as a punishment for my unspeakable wrong, but Lina never knew about my sin. It's the only thing I'm proud of in my whole life, that my sister never knew. I shielded her from that.

" 'Maybe he will forgive me and let me come back someday,' Lina said just before she went out the door, but we both knew that wouldn't happen. I went out on the porch to watch her climb up on the extra horse Daniel had brought. She wore a red dress that she gathered up between her legs. The sun was bright that day, and the red flashed in the sun with her golden hair.

"I cried as I made corn bread for Father's supper. It was the first night of my life sentence in prison. After a while, I quit crying, but I never quit suffering. It was the life I chose.

"That night Lina left, Father came in just when the grandfather clock struck six times. He opened the door and found Lina gone.

" 'She's dead to us. Do you hear me, daughter? Dead!' he thundered. 'She has defied me, and she has made her choice!' He pounded his big fist on the kitchen table, shaking the plates I had set out.

"He ate a huge meal: ham, squash, corn bread, and fried apples. It's the smell of those apples that stuck with me. Even today I can't stand the smell of cooked apples." Portia paused to breathe deeply and to think.

"She died later, then?" Ophelia asked.

"Probably Father wouldn't even have read the letter Lina's mother-in-law wrote to tell us about her death if it hadn't been in an envelope edged in black. Father read the letter aloud to me. His voice never changed one bit as he said the words, and he tossed the letter into the flames of the fireplace. Just tossed it in to burn, then sat down to eat his dinner.

"But Daniel came back. This time he didn't try to hide, just walked into the house one evening while we were at the supper table. He had a gun, and his eyes were different.

" 'I'll shoot you if I have to,' he said to my father. 'I came for Portia. It was Lina's last wish. "Get my sister," she said just before she died. "Please get my sister out of there." That's what I aim to do.'

"I couldn't look at Daniel, couldn't bear to see the grief on his face. I couldn't look at my father, either. I could never bear to look at my father. I just kept my eyes on the table in front of me, and I said. 'My place is here.'

" 'Please, Portia, do it for Carolina. My mother wants you to live with her.'

"I just shook my head. Daniel made a sort of sobbing sound, and I knew he was crying. He turned and walked out. I never looked up."

"How about the baby? Did your sister's baby live?"

"No. The baby died too, but that child was Lina's second-born. Her first child did not die at birth." Portia held out her hand toward the girl. "Come. Take my hand and come off that rock, and I will tell you something that no other soul has ever known."

"No. I'm going to jump. I should have already jumped before you got here." There was a silence then, and for a time only the sound of the river could be heard.

"You must not jump." *Don't plead,* Portia told herself. *Stay calm.* "Please don't let me see another golden girl die."

"But you didn't see your sister die."

"No," said Portia, and her voice came out cold, cold across the years of silence. "I saw her child die, a beautiful golden baby."

Portia thought she saw Ophelia's body shift toward her, toward the bank. She took a breath and then went on. "You think you've done wrong? You think you've got blood on your hands? Oh, child, listen to my 'tale unfold.' "

"From *Hamlet,*" said Ophelia. "The ghost said those words, 'a tale unfold.' "

"Yes," said Portia. "You're a good student of Shakespeare."

"What happened? What did you do wrong?"

"The baby was born in the woods. Father didn't know. He never knew a thing about it. I delivered that baby with my own hands. I was fourteen years old, and I delivered that baby. I loved it too, loved that little golden girl almost as much as I loved my sister. Almost, but not quite as much."

"So what went wrong? Why did the baby die?"

"It was a summer night, the night of July 19, 1921."

"The date on this rock!"

This time Portia was sure that Ophelia moved slightly toward her. "I let my sister hold the baby before I brought it down here to the water. I planned to wash her with a cloth, then wrap her in a towel."

Ophelia edged a little closer, and Portia took a deep breath, ready to go on. "I sat right there." She pointed with her cane. "Right there beside the water. I dipped the cloth in the water, and I washed that beautiful little body. I talked to her, too, talked about how much her mother loved her and about how much I loved her. The moon shone on her, and I could see her blond hair and blue eyes. She would have had curls, like her mother. I loved that baby, but I loved her mother more. I knew what Father would do to Lina if he ever saw that baby. I held her there beside the water, and then suddenly I held her in the water. For a minute, I looked at her there in the water, and then, without planning to do it, I lowered her."

"What?" Ophelia moved again. "You lowered her into the water?"

"No," said the old woman, and her voice came out so tired. "Under the water. I drowned that baby in this very river. Held her sweet body under this water until her arms and legs stopped moving."

Portia held out her hand again. "I've told no one, not ever. I buried her here, dug in the soft dirt with my hands, then dragged this flat rock over the top of the grave. Later I carved the date. I wanted a testament to the baby's life and to my sin. I went back to Lina and told her the baby died, that she was dead by the time I had reached the river."

"You killed the baby? You drowned it?" In Ophelia's voice Portia could hear the sound of tears about to burst out.

"I did, and I've paid for it all my days. So you see, child, you've no blood on your hands, not compared to mine. Come off that rock now, and let's go home. Let's go home and help each other."

"No." Ophelia moved away from Portia. "What you've told me doesn't change anything. Your guilt doesn't make it any easier for me to live. I just don't want to go on." She turned away. "You'd better leave now. If you don't want to see me drown, you'd better leave."

A desperate plan began to form in Portia's mind. She would create a diversion.

"I won't go home without you." Portia stepped toward the girl and closer to the edge. First she deliberately dropped her walking stick on the rock; then, arms waving, her body went into the water.

The scream came out just as Portia's head went under, but her mind still worked. *Remember this water, remember from when you were young,* she told herself. *Swim, swim as you did in those childhood days.*

Portia McKay held her breath and fought the strong river. Her heavy coat got snagged on an underwater branch and held her beneath the rushing water. Her fingers finally found the buttons. She struggled to pull off the garment before she ran out of air in her lungs. One sleeve took longer than the other, and Portia tugged with desperation, her lungs about to burst. Finally the coat floated away, and Portia broke through the water's surface.

"Help me, child," she screamed, and she fought to keep the river from carrying her farther from the rock. "Use my stick."

"Here." Ophelia grabbed the cane and held it out to the dark form in the water, but it wouldn't reach. She dropped to the cold rock, lay on her stomach, stretched as far as she could, and held out the cane.

This time Portia could almost reach it. "Swim," yelled Ophelia. "You can swim that far."

The icy water slapped at Portia, and the roar seemed to pull her into it. She felt tired, too tired to fight for even a few more inches.

Ophelia waved the stick. "Here, Miss McKay. Just try, please. I don't want you to die. It'd be my fault. Please!"

The words came to Portia over the sound of the river, and Portia did try. With one great surge of strength, she reached out to swim against the water. Just a few inches, not more than two feet. She sucked in a deep breath and, face in the water, struggled until she felt the cane against her head.

"Grab on!" Ophelia called, and again Portia obeyed the voice.

She felt her body being pulled through the water toward the rock with the carved date. "Hold on to the rock," Ophelia called as she grasped Portia's arms. "We've got to get you up here out of the water. Climb."

"Too tired." One of Portia's hands slipped from the rock, but Ophelia held tight to her arms.

The girl pulled. Portia's body moved up slightly, but it slid back down into the water. "Come on," Ophelia screamed. "You've got to help me. Please! I need you to help me."

Portia started to crawl. Holding on to the rock, she used her knee to push herself up. "That's the way," Ophelia said, and she gave another great heave upward. "You're out, Miss McKay," she said, "but we can't stop here." She looked down into the woman's face. "Miss McKay? Open your eyes!"

Portia McKay did not respond. "Don't die now," Ophelia begged, and she dragged the woman from the rock to the riverbank. "Here." She took off her coat and spread it across the wet woman, pausing just long enough to feel what she was sure was a slight moving up and down of Miss McKay's chest.

"I'll be right back," she yelled over her shoulder. "I've got to get help." She ran then, ran and slipped and ran again. Breathing hard, she had almost made it to the top of the hill when her foot slid on the icy grass. Her body tumbled all the way to the bottom.

Ophelia got up and, without waiting to brush herself off, began to move again. The distance to the Reynoldses' house had once seemed short, but now she felt each rock. She wiped the falling ice from her eyes and hurried down the road.

When finally the lights from the house came into view, Ophelia, exhausted, let herself lean for just a second against a tree. Then, pushing her body away from the trunk, she rushed, screaming, toward the light.

Inside the door, Ophelia collapsed on the floor. "Help me," she yelled.

"Mercy, mercy! What's wrong?" Bernice Reynolds came running from the kitchen and gathered Ophelia in her arms.

After Mrs. Reynolds called the ambulance, Ophelia gathered blankets. She was going out the door when Mrs. Reynolds called, "Wait!" and hurried to hand the girl a thermos. "Hot coffee," she said. "Be careful, honey."

"I'm going to the hospital with her," Ophelia yelled as she ran. How long would it take her to get back? she wondered. Eight minutes? Ten? Would Miss McKay still be breathing?

She was at the path now, edging her way down the hill. "Slow down," she told herself, but the warning came too late. Her body tumbled down the hill, the coffee thermos flying from her hands. She held tight to the rolled blankets, and they protected her when she slammed into a tree trunk.

Ophelia decided to leave the coffee for now and rushed on. Miss McKay had not moved. Ophelia could see her long body on the ice-covered grass.

She spread one blanket and rolled the old woman onto it. Then she covered her with the other. As she worked, she talked. "I'm here now, Miss McKay," she said, "and help is coming."

The woman did not stir. Ophelia did not take time to feel for breathing until she had the woman covered. With a shaking arm, she reached out to put her hand over the heart. "Your heart's still beating," she said, and she began to cry. Then she lifted the blanket, lay down close to the old woman, and pulled the cover over them both.

While they waited for the ambulance, Ophelia talked. She told about the foster homes, about the cruel things kids had done at school, and about the way she had learned to count things to save her sanity.

Finally, Ophelia saw the ambulance lights. She jumped up and, yelling, "Here! Here!" she scrambled up the hill.

It took a while for the men to get up the hill with the stretcher. Ophelia wanted to be beside them, holding Miss McKay's hand, but she knew she would only be in the way. Instead, she waited at the top, pacing back and forth.

They were putting her inside, hooking her to something, when one man said to the other, "Poor old thing. Doesn't have any family, not one living soul to care for her."

"You're wrong," Ophelia interrupted. "She's got me." She climbed into the ambulance to hold the woman's hand.

"It's shock," the doctor told Ophelia when he came out of the examining room to talk to her. "She's old, but she's strong. I believe she'll be okay."

Ophelia believed the doctor, but she stayed beside her friend all night, only dozing in a chair. In the morning, Portia McKay opened her eyes. "We've got to go back to that rock," she said. "I want another date added, the date you saved my life."

"And you saved mine," the girl said.

"An important day," Portia said, and she went back to sleep.

———

Bernice Reynolds and Ophelia took Portia home from the hospital. "I just don't know why you won't have a phone," Bernice complained as she helped settle Portia in the backseat. "Just plain too stubborn for your own good, if you ask me." She pulled the blanket over Portia's knees.

"Well, you know, I believe you're right about that. Will you call the phone people for me?"

"I can't believe it," said Bernice, and her eyes grew large.

When they stopped in front of the old house, Ophelia stared out at it from the car window. *It looks different somehow*, she thought, *more friendly*. "Lean on me," she told Portia as they walked toward the door. "And by the way, I'm staying with you for a few days."

"But your schooling?" Portia protested.

"Her social worker says it's okay. I'll pick up her assignments for her," said Bernice, and she hurried ahead to open the door.

For a while Portia rested, but after Bernice was gone, she got up and moved slowly from room to room. Ophelia followed. Portia paused, touching a teapot, the lace curtains, and books on the shelf. At the rocking chair, Portia reached out to set the chair in motion. "The walls have fallen," she said softly. Then she turned to Ophelia. "My prison is gone." She shook her head in wonder and dropped into the chair.

"What do you mean?" Ophelia moved to stand beside the woman, and she bent close to hear the soft answer.

"I've made my peace," she said. "I went into the river, and my peace is made."

Ophelia dropped beside her and leaned her head into the woman's lap. Portia stroked the girl's hair. "When you are strong again, will you go with me on the bus back to Deer Run?" Ophelia asked. "I want to see my house again, and I want to go to the cemetery."

"Oh, child," said the woman. "We'll go, but not on any bus. I'll hire a driver and a car."

That evening Ophelia read to Portia. "Let's read something lighter," she said, and Portia suggested Dickens's *Martin Chuzzlewit*.

The next day when Bernice Reynolds came to check on Portia and Ophelia, she found them at the kitchen table having a ham-and-eggs supper.

"Well, I could eat a little something," Bernice said when Portia invited her to join them. While they ate, Bernice shared her news. "When I called the school today to say I'd come for your work, they told me one of your friends had volunteered to bring it." She peered closely at Ophelia. "What friend would that be, honey?"

Ophelia shrugged her shoulders. "Don't know for sure," she said, but she smiled. She smiled again when she saw Mark Haines coming up the walk with books under his arm.

Ophelia opened the door. "Come in," she said.

"I brought your books and stuff." Mark stepped inside. "Are you okay and everything?" He scratched at his hand and shifted his feet.

Ophelia had never seen Mark nervous. She took the books. "Thank you," she said. "I'm all right, just helping out a friend for a few days." She smiled at Mark.

"You don't mind that I came, do you?"

"I'm glad."

"You are?" His St. Bernard puppy smile was back. "Well, then will you go out with me sometime?"

"I'll be back at my foster home in four days. I'll ask then." She rearranged the books in her arms. "I think it will be okay. Mrs. Reynolds is good to me."

"Great! Will you be back to school then, in four days?"

Ophelia nodded. "Yes."

"I'll be waiting for you when you get off the bus. We'll walk in together. Okay?"

"Okay," said Ophelia. She looked over her shoulder toward Mrs. McKay, who seemed to be asleep on the couch.

"Take your friend for a walk, why don't you?" said the woman without opening her eyes. "He might like to see our spot on the river."

"Sure I would." Mark stepped toward the door.

At first they moved without talking. "I like living around here," Ophelia said when they were on the road. "I like it a lot."

"Good, I'm relieved. I hated it when you talked about leaving." Mark bent to pick up a rock and rolled it about in his hand.

Ophelia stopped where the path led down to the river. "It's down this way," she said. "There's a big rock by the water." She looked up at Mark to see if he seemed interested, but he had already taken a step from the road. He held a branch back from the path so that Ophelia could get by.

The river did not rush quite as much as it had on the night that Mrs. McKay fell in, but still the sound made it necessary to speak loudly. "Here's the rock." Ophelia stood still and looked. The late-afternoon sun left shadows on the water, and a big, fallen branch floated in the middle of the stream.

"This is a nice spot," said Mark.

"Yes," said Ophelia, "the river makes it really peaceful." She smiled at Mark, and she did not pull away when he took her hand.